KT-431-199

www.hants.gov.uk/library

Tel: 0300 555 1387

CLAIMING HIS HIDDEN HEIR

CAROL MARINELLI

MILLS & BOON

First Published in Great Britain 2018
by Mills & Boon, an imprint of HarperCollins*Publishers*
1 London Bridge Street, London, SE1 9GF

© 2018 Carol Marinelli

ISBN: 978-0-263-93436-6

MIX
Paper from
responsible sources
FSC® C007454

This book is produced from independently certified FSC™ paper
to ensure responsible forest management.
For more information visit www.harpercollins.co.uk/green.

Printed and bound in Spain
by CPI, Barcelona

For my great friend Frances Housden

An inspiring woman and wonderful writer.

Love always

Carol xxx

PROLOGUE

HE WOULD NOT be hiring Cecelia Andrews.

Property magnate Luka Kargas had already decided that Candidate Number Two would be his new personal assistant.

'Ms Andrews is here for her interview,' Hannah, his current PA, informed him.

'There's no need for me to meet her,' Luka responded. 'I've decided to go with Candidate Two.'

'Luka!' Hannah reproached, a little braver now that she was leaving. 'At least have the decency to see her. She's been through two extensive interviews with me, and as well as that it's pouring outside. She had to come across London in the middle of a storm.'

'Not interested,' Luka said, because he didn't buy into sob stories. 'It's a waste of my time.'

And a slice of Luka's time was precious indeed.

But then Luka suddenly remembered that Ms Andrews had been personally recommended by Justin, a contact he wanted to keep onside.

'Fine, send her in,' Luka said, deciding to see her briefly but then to get rid of her as soon as he could.

Impatient fingers drummed the desk as he waited, and then Candidate Three was shown in.

'Ms Andrews.' Luka stood and shook her right hand, noticing that on her left she wore an engagement ring.

Nothing would induce him to hire her, for she would have to have the most patient fiancé in the world to tolerate the ridiculous hours she would have to devote to him.

And *everyone* knew his reputation.

He just had to give her a few minutes of his time so he could tell Justin that he had interviewed her but gone with another candidate.

'Please,' he said. 'Take a seat.'

Cecelia knew that although he had called her Ms Andrews he was awaiting correction and an invitation to call her by her first name.

There would be no such invitation to do so.

Ms Andrews would do just fine, Cecelia had decided.

She had read about him, thoroughly researched him, and even been told by his current PA during two prolonged interviews about his bad-boy ways.

'You would have to deal with his girlfriends, or rather his exes,' Hannah had explained. 'It can be quite a juggling act at times. Luka works hard all week and then works just as hard breaking hearts at the weekend.'

Cecelia had seen it all before, and not just through her work. She abhorred the rich, debauched kind of lifestyle he led and with good reason—her mother, Harriet, had lived and died the same way.

Still, Luka Kargas's morals were his own concern, not hers. Cecelia had her sights set on working for royalty and he was a step in the right direction, that was all.

'He has a yacht, currently moored in Xanero,' Hannah had said.

'That's where he's from?' Cecelia checked, although she had found that out in her research.

'Yes, though you won't be expected to travel there with him and you won't be involved with the family business there. Luka keeps that strictly separate.'

She would not be falling for him, Cecelia had reassured both his incumbent PA and herself. The only thing the career-minded Cecelia wanted from Luka Kargas was his name on her résumé and the glowing reference that, after a year's hard work, he would surely provide.

But now she had finally met him, and as his long olive fingers had closed around hers, the very sensible Cecelia's conviction that she would not be attracted to him in the least had wavered somewhat.

'Hannah said you got caught in the storm,' Luka frowned.

The skies had darkened just over an hour ago.

Luka, from his vantage point of the fortieth floor, had watched the black clouds gather and roll over London.

Candidate Two had arrived drenched and had asked Hannah for a ten-minute delay before proceeding with the interview.

Usually that would have been enough to ensure a black mark against her name but, having watched the storm himself, Luka had accepted the excuse and the rather bedraggled candidate.

Cecelia Andrews was far from bedraggled, though.

She wore a dark grey suit that was immaculate, her blonde hair, worn up, was sleek and smooth, while her make-up was both discreet and in place.

Hannah had insinuated that a drowned rat sat in the entrance yet the woman who sat before him was far from that.

'I got caught up in the storm,' Cecelia said, 'but I wasn't caught out—I heeded the warnings.'

And she might want to start heeding them now, she thought, for the impact of him on her senses was like nothing she had ever known.

He wore a dark suit and tie and his crisp white shirt accentuated his olive skin; he hadn't shaved that morning.

The air in the room had changed, as if the charge that had lit the sky for the past hour had joined them.

Luka Kargas was everything her aunt had warned her about, and though she had told herself she could handle it, and that there was no way she could ever be attracted to someone like him, Cecelia hadn't allowed for the impact of Luka close up.

They skipped through the formalities, both determined to get this over and done with and move on with the day.

'Hannah will have explained that the hours are long,' Luka said.

'She did.'

'Sixteen-hour days at times.'

'Yes.' Cecelia nodded.

'And there's an awful lot of travel,' Luka said. 'Though for all that the working week is hell, you do get every weekend off.'

She smiled a tight, slightly disbelieving smile.

'You do,' Luka said, as he read those full lips. 'Come Friday night, the entire weekend is yours.'

'Though I'm guessing I wouldn't be out of here by five p.m.?'

'No,' he said. 'Usually around ten.'

So not really the entire weekend to herself, Cecelia thought as his black eyes scanned through her paperwork. 'Why are you finishing up with Justin?'

'Because I didn't want to live in Dubai.'

'I go there a lot,' Luka said, 'which would mean, by default, so would you.'

'That's fine. I just don't want to live there,' Cecelia said, and she knew, she just knew, he was alluding to the fact she had a fiancé whose needs would have impacted on her decision.

He was right.

Gordon wouldn't consider it.

'Do you speak Greek?' he asked.

'No,' Cecelia said, suddenly hoping it was a prerequisite for the role and that this torture would therefore come to an end. It was torture because her stomach seemed to be folding in on itself and she all of a sudden could feel the weight of her breasts. She had never had such a violent reaction to another person, though of course it was one-sided.

Luka Kargas looked thoroughly bored.

'Do you speak any other languages?' he asked.

'Some French,' Cecelia said, even though she spoke it very well and had both lived and worked in France for a year.

Anyway, he didn't want her French, whether a little or a lot of it, for he screwed up his nose.

Good, because Cecelia had now decided that she did not want this job.

She liked safe, and for very good reasons.

Cecelia liked her world ordered, and ten minutes alone with Luka Kargas had just rocked hers.

His black eyes were mesmerising and his brusque indifference had her re-crossing her legs.

Until this moment, sex had been a perfectly pleasant experience, if sometimes a bit of a chore.

Now, though, she sat across from a man who made her think of it.

Actually sit and think about torrid, impromptu sex at two p.m. on a Monday afternoon, and that could never do.

'Ms Andrews...'

'Cecelia,' she corrected, but only because she didn't want to sound like some uptight spinster.

And she wasn't.

She was engaged to be married, and right now she found herself desperately trying to hold onto that thought.

Oh, this really would never do!

'Cecelia.' He nodded. 'I see that you don't have any real experience in the hospitality industry.'

'No, I don't,' Cecelia said. 'Not a jot.'

'A jot?' His black eyes looked up and met her green ones and she saw that his were not actually black but the deepest of browns.

'I don't have any experience in the hospitality industry, none at all.'

'And I note that you wear an engagement ring.'

'Excuse me...' Cecelia frowned '...but you can't comment on that.'

He waved his hand dismissively.

Luka read her emergency contact and saw that it wasn't her fiancé but, in fact, her aunt.

And she intrigued him a touch. '*Are* you engaged?'

'Yes.' Cecelia bristled. 'Not that it's any of your business.'

'Cecelia, if you are considering working for me, then you might as well know from the outset that I am not known for my political correctness. I'll tell it to you straight—I don't want a PA who is in the throes of planning a big wedding, neither I don't want someone who is going to have to dash off at six because her fiancé is sulking.'

Cecelia's jaw tightened because at times Gordon did just that.

'Mr Kargas, my personal life is not your concern and, let me assure you, it never will be.'

Never, because she was not taking the job!

He heard the double meaning behind her words and almost smiled but then checked himself.

'Come over here,' he said, and stood up and headed to the floor-to-ceiling windows.

It was like no interview she had ever experienced before, Cecelia thought as she stood and walked over to join him.

Gosh, he was tall.

And he smelt as if he had bathed in bergamot with a testosterone undertone.

'See the view,' Luka said.

'It's amazing.' Cecelia nodded, looking out across a gleaming, wet and shiny London. The grey skies were starting to clear and black clouds were lined with silver but there was no rainbow that she could see.

'It's all yours,' Luka said, and Cecelia frowned. 'When you finish on a Friday, right up to Monday morning the world out there is your oyster.' Then he looked over at her. 'But when you're here…'

He expected devotion. Cecelia got his meaning.

'When can you start?' Luka asked.

Before she declined, Cecelia took a deep breath and thought of the perks of this job—a salary that was almost twice her current one, endless travel and the Kargas name on her résumé for ever.

And then she thought of the pitfalls.

Sixty-hour weeks spent beside this stunning man.

Her attraction to him was as unexpected as it was unsettling.

She actually didn't know what to do.

'I'd like some time to think about it,' Cecelia said in response to his offer.

'Well, I'm looking for someone who trusts their own instincts and can make prompt decisions.'

Luka now wanted her working for him.

She had impressed him when he had not expected to be impressed, yet something told him that if she walked out of the door Cecelia Andrews would not be coming back.

He could *feel* her hesitation.

And because he was Luka Kargas he knew when to push, and how. 'So, I'll ask again, when can you start, Cecelia?'

Never! Her instincts screamed.

Yet she had so badly wanted this job and the challenge it would bring and, though he was undoubtedly attractive, Cecelia knew herself well enough to be certain she would never get involved with anyone at work.

'Now,' Cecelia said, shocked at her own decision. 'I can start now.'

'Then welcome aboard.'

And as he shook her hand, Cecelia told herself she could handle it.

CHAPTER ONE

LUKA, AFTER CAREFUL consideration I've decided…

Waking just before her alarm went off, Cecelia lay listening to the hiss of bus doors opening on the street outside her London flat and working out how best to resign.

And when to do it?

Did she get it over and done with in the morning? Or wait until the end of the day to tell him that she would not be renewing her contract?

Most people would say she was mad to quit.

The pay was amazing, the travel wonderful, if exhausting, but in the eleven months she had worked for Luka, Cecelia had hit the limit on her primness radar.

He was a playboy in the extreme.

And that wasn't some vague, unsourced opinion.

It was fact.

Cecelia ran his diary after all!

Quite simply, she couldn't do it any more and so on Friday, as Luka had headed to the rooftop to swan off in his chopper for a debauched weekend in France, Cecelia had reached for her phone and accepted a six-month contract as personal assistant to an esteemed and elderly foreign diplomat.

While the money and perks would be worse in her

new job, the peace of mind it would bring was, to Cecelia, worth its weight in gold.

Only as she reached for her phone to check the time did Cecelia see the date and remember that it was her birthday.

There was never much fuss made of it and she had long since told herself to get over that fact. Her aunt and uncle, who had raised her since the age of eight, simply didn't bother with such things and before she had died, neither had her mother.

She saw that a message had come in overnight from Luka.

Shan't be in today, Cece. Cancel my meetings and I'll call you later.

Cecelia ground her teeth at the annoying shortening of her name that she had repeatedly asked him to stop using. But then she frowned, because in the eleven months that she had worked for Luka he had never taken a day off. Luka had a phenomenal workload yet never missed a beat. But now, on the one day she really needed to speak to him, he wasn't going to be there.

Cecelia wanted her resignation handed in and sorted, and for her time with Luka to be over. As well as that he had an important meeting with Mr Garcia and his entourage in NYC later today. Although it was an online meeting, it had been incredibly hard to set up and it was going to be extremely messy to cancel.

Despite the absence of her boss—in fact, *because* of the absence of her boss—today was shaping up to be an exceptionally busy one, and so Cecelia forced herself up and out of bed.

She showered quickly and began to get ready.

Her routines were set in stone and, despite the extensive travel and odd hours required by her job, there were certain things that never changed. She could be in Florence, New York, or home in London but these things remained—her clothes were set out the night before, as was her breakfast, which she ate before tackling her hair.

Routines were vital to Cecelia's sense of well-being, for during the first eight years of her life, when she had lived with her mother, chaos had been the only certainty.

The reddish fire to Cecelia's strawberry blonde mane had, courtesy of foils, been dimmed to a neutral blonde. She smoothed and sleeked out her long curls and then tied them back into a neat, low ponytail.

Next, Cecelia applied her make-up.

She didn't wear much, but as Luka's PA it was expected that she was always well turned out.

It wasn't always the case. A famous actress she had once worked for had insisted that Cecelia wear no make-up whatsoever as well as extremely plain clothing. With another employer, for practical reasons, her wardrobe had mainly consisted of boots and jeans.

Cecelia's skin was pale and needed just a dash of blusher to liven it up. She added a coat of mascara to her lashes, which enhanced her deep green eyes, but, as she did so, a rather bitchy voice coming from the radio caught her attention.

'What on earth did she expect, getting mixed up with Luka Kargas?'

Cecelia stabbed herself in the eye with the mascara wand at the sound of her boss's name.

It wasn't so much that it was a surprise to hear Luka mentioned, more an annoyance that even at seven a.m.

and alone in her bedroom *still* there was no escape from him.

Luka was extremely prominent and, although his name often graced the finance reports, his antics and bad-boy ways were regularly discussed in the tabloids and on the news.

They were having a field day discussing him now!

It would seem that he had used every last second of the weekend to create his own particular brand of havoc. A wild party had taken place aboard his yacht, currently moored off the coast of Nice, on Friday.

Cecelia sat at her dressing table, lips pursed as she heard that the raucous celebrations had continued on to Paris, where Luka and selected guests had hit the casinos. Now it was a case of tears *after* bedtime for some supermodel who had hoped that things might be different between herself and Luka.

Well, more fool her, then, Cecelia thought.

Everyone knew Luka's track record with women.

But they didn't really know Luka—there was a private side to him that no one, and certainly not his PA, had access to.

From what Cecelia could glean, Luka had led a very privileged life. His father owned a luxurious resort in Xanero. The famed Kargas restaurant there was now the flagship venue of its own very exclusive brand in several countries. Luka, though, focused more on expanding the hotel side of things and lived life very much in the fast lane. He dated at whim and discarded with ease and all too often it was Cecelia mopping up the tears or fielding calls from scorned lovers.

Yes, he was a playboy in the extreme.

And he unsettled her so.

Cecelia had once glimpsed that life.

Her mother Harriet's death had been intensely embarrassing for her well-to-do family for she had died as she'd lived and had gone out on a high—knickers down and with the proverbial silver spoon up her nose.

Harriet had left behind a daughter with whom no one had quite known what to do. Her father's name did not appear on the birth certificate and Cecelia had glimpsed him just once in her life.

And she never wanted to see him again.

Cecelia's staid aunt and uncle, who had always sniffed in disapproval at Harriet's rather bohemian existence, had, on her death, taken in the child. With tangled curls and sparkling green eyes, little Cecelia had been a mini replica of her mother, but in looks only.

The little girl had craved routine.

In fact, it had been a very young Cecelia who had kept any semblance of order in her mother's life.

She had put out her own school uniform and taken money from her mother's purse to ensure there was food, and she'd always got herself up in the morning and made her own way to school.

After an unconventional start, Cecelia now lived a very conventional life and was efficient and ordered. Even though she travelled the globe with her work, she was generally in bed by ten on weekdays and eleven at weekends.

She had perfectly nice friends, though none close enough to remember her birthday, and this time last year she had been engaged.

Gordon and the break-up had been the only problem she had caused for her aunt and uncle, who could not fathom why she might end things with such a perfectly decent man.

It hadn't been Gordon's fault, and she had told him so when she'd ended it.

It was bloody Luka's!

Though of course Cecelia hadn't told Gordon that.

Still, there wasn't time to dwell on it this morning.

She pulled on her flesh-coloured underwear and then glanced out of the window where the sun split a very blue sky, and found she simply could not face putting on the navy linen suit that she had laid out last night.

To hell with it!

Given that Luka wouldn't be in the office today, and that she wouldn't now be sitting in on meetings, Cecelia made an unplanned diversion to her wardrobe.

She wasn't exactly blinded by colour. But there was the dress she had bought to wear to a friend's wedding she had recently attended.

It had been a rare impulse purchase.

It was a pale cream halter neck, which Cecelia had decided as soon as she'd left the boutique was too close to white and might offend the bride.

She loved it, though, and, maybe because it was her birthday, she decided to wear it.

While it showed rather too much of her back and arms, she took care of that with the pale lemon, sheer, bolero-style cardigan she had bought on the same day.

The dress was mid-calf-length so she didn't bother with stockings, and then she tied on some espadrilles.

Yes, perhaps because Cecelia knew she would soon be leaving Kargas Holdings she was finally starting to relax.

As she closed the front door to her flat, Cecelia decided that despite Luka's absence she would still be giving in her notice today. It would be far easier to do it over the phone or online.

'You're looking very summery,' Mrs Dawson, her very nosy neighbour, said as she passed her in the hall. 'Off to work?'

'I am.'

The pale lemon bolero didn't even make it past the escalators to the underground. It was hot and oppressive and as she stood, holding a rail, she saw that Luka's weekend escapades had made headlines on the newspaper a commuter held.

She looked at the photo beneath the headline. It was of Luka on the deck of his yacht moving in on a sophisticated, dark-skinned beauty. His naked chest and thick black hair were dripping water over the woman and though their bodies did not touch it was an incredibly intimate shot.

Cecelia tore her eyes from the picture and stared fixedly ahead but that image of him seemed to dance on the blacked-out windows of the Tube.

Having left the underground, Cecelia walked towards the prominent high-rise building that housed Kargas Holdings. She smiled at the doorman and then entered the foyer and took the elevator. She had a special pass that allowed her to access the fortieth floor, which was Luka's in its entirety.

There weren't just offices and meeting rooms, there was also a gym and pool, though Cecelia couldn't recall him using them—they were more a perk for the staff.

And there was a suite that was every bit as luxurious and as serviced as any five-star hotel. When in London, Luka often slept there when he chose to work through the night or had a particularly early morning flight.

Yes, it was his world that she entered, but knowing that he wasn't there meant Cecelia breathed more easily today.

It was just before eight and it would seem that she had beaten Bridgette, the receptionist, to work. There were a couple of cleaners polishing windows and vacuuming and the florists had arrived, as they did each morning to tend the floral displays.

Cecelia made a coffee from the espresso machine before heading to her desk that was housed in a large area outside Luka's vast office.

The gatekeeper, Luka called her at times, though she felt rather more like a security guard at others.

As well as greeting his clients and guests, Cecelia was the final hurdle for his scorned lovers to negotiate if they somehow made it past the security in place downstairs.

Occasionally it happened, though generally Cecelia fielded them by phone.

And there it was again, springing to mind—the sudden image of him, wet from the ocean and dripping water, and Cecelia shook her head as if to clear it.

She hung her little cardigan on a stand and was just about to take a seat when his voice caught her completely unawares.

'Is that coffee for me, Cece?'

Cecelia swung around and there, strolling out of his office, was Luka. Apart from being unshaven there was little evidence of his wild weekend on display. He wore black pants and a white fitted shirt that showed off his toned body and his thick black hair, which, though perhaps a little tousled, still fell into perfect shape.

And he was not supposed to be here.

'I thought you weren't coming in today,' Cecelia said.

'Why would you think that?'

'Because you texted me in the middle of the night and told me you weren't.'

'So I did.'

He looked at the usually poised and formal Cece caught unawares. To many it might seem no big deal—she was simply holding a coffee and wearing a summer dress. Usually she was buttoned to the neck in navy or black, but it wasn't just her clothing that was different today.

'Thanks,' he said, and took from her hand the coffee she had made.

'It's got sugar in it,' she warned as she took a seat at her desk, 'and, please, it's Cecelia, not Cece.'

'Habit,' he said.

'Well, it's a very annoying one.'

Good, Luka thought.

Her cool demeanour incensed him.

His choice of name for her was deliberate, for he loved to provoke a reaction, even if it was only mild.

'How was your weekend?' she asked politely, pretending of course that she had heard nothing whatsoever about it.

'Much the same as the last,' he answered, and then came over behind Cecelia's desk and, to her intense annoyance, he lowered himself so that his bottom was beside her computer. 'Do you ever get bored?' he asked.

'Not really,' Cecelia lied, for she had realised she had been bored with Gordon.

He had also worked in the City and they had fallen into a pattern of meeting for drinks on Wednesday, allowing time to catch up with friends on a Friday. It had generally just been the two of them on a Saturday, followed by a vague hint of an orgasm that night and generally a boring drive on Sunday with a pub lunch somewhere.

And then perhaps another anti-climactic tryst that night.

It hadn't been Gordon's fault.

Cecelia held back in sex just as she held back in life.

In fact, the fault lay with the man now lounging against her desk, for he had opened her eyes to sensations that should surely remain unexplored.

Oh, she should never have taken the job, Cecelia thought as Luka persisted with a conversation she would rather draw to a close.

'But don't you ever get tired of doing the same old thing?' he asked.

'I like the same old things,' Cecelia answered.

He glanced at her neat, ordered desk and knew that the inside of her drawers would look exactly the same.

And then, just to annoy her, just to provoke *some* reaction, he picked up her little pottery jar that held her pens and things and moved it to the other side of her desk. 'Live a little.'

'No, thank you.' She smiled grimly and moved the jar back where it belonged. As she did so he got the scent of freshly washed hair.

That was it.

Cecelia didn't wear perfume; there were no undertones that he could note, and not just in her scent.

She was impossible to read, unlike any woman Luka had ever met. He had long ago given up flirting with her—the disapproval in her eyes kind of ruined the fun.

And as reckless as he was, Luka only ever played with the willing.

'You look nice,' he told her, and he felt the scold of her slight frown for daring to comment on something personal. Cecelia kept things very strictly business, yet she responded politely.

'Thank you.'

But Luka did not leave it there. 'You're wearing a dress.'

'That's very observant of you, Luka.'

'I'm just mentioning it because you don't usually.'

'Well, it's been a long, warm weekend. I couldn't face wearing a suit.'

'No, but—'

'Luka,' Cecelia interrupted him, 'if you have an issue with me dressing more casually than normal, then please just say so and it won't happen again.'

'I have no issue with you wearing a dress.'

'Then there's nothing to discuss.'

'Are you sure about that?' Luka said. He hadn't intended to address this today but clearly the moment was upon them.

'What I wear—' Cecelia started to say, but then Luka cut in.

'Do you have another *dental appointment* today, Cecelia?' His voice had changed and he delivered his words with a threatening edge by using her correct name. 'A final interview perhaps?'

He was rather certain that she was leaving, and more certain now because to her pale cheeks there came a very rare flush.

PAs came and went.

Luka was very used to that.

He was an exceptionally demanding boss and was aware that few could keep up with his impossible schedule for very long.

Usually all he required was for the incumbent PA to train the next one to standard before she left and ensure that the handover was seamless.

That Cecelia might be about to leave, though, brought a sense of disquiet like nothing he had known.

He liked her in his life, Luka realised, and he didn't want her to be gone. But three prolonged dental appointments in recent weeks had served as ominous signs, and he'd been certain of it when she had avoided discussing the renewal of her contract.

'Is there something you've been meaning to tell me?' he asked.

'Actually, yes.' She took a breath and then glanced over at the sound of the elevator door opening and saw that Bridgette had arrived.

Cecelia did not want an audience for this.

'Would it be possible to have a word in private?'

'Of course,' Luka said. 'You know my door is always closed.' When she didn't smile at his little joke he stood from the desk. 'Come on through.'

Luka decided he would have to talk her out of it.

And he knew just how to do it.

CHAPTER TWO

IT FELT LIKE a very long walk to his office.

Luka led the way and Cecelia actually felt a little sick because she still wasn't certain that it was the right thing to do.

Cecelia was very career minded and knew that by resigning she was throwing an amazing role away—Luka's empire was rapidly expanding, with hotels in New York City and Singapore on the cards, and to be a part of it would be amazing on her résumé.

But as he held open the door and she walked in, Cecelia knew she had little choice but to leave.

She could feel his eyes on her back.

On her skin.

They most certainly were.

Cecelia had the drabbest wardrobe he had ever seen.

Granted, she was always groomed and elegant, but Luka had long ago decided that she could make a modest outfit out of a handkerchief.

Not so today.

On the day she would tell him that she was leaving, he got the first glimpse of her spine.

Her back was incredibly pale, and he wondered if she should check her Vitamin D levels because he was sure that body rarely, if ever, saw the sun.

Luka had run into her out of work once and she'd been dressed in much the same monotonous, drab tones.

It had been at a museum exhibition a couple of weeks after she had started working for him, and not *quite* by accident. Luka had heard her discussing going with her fiancé and he'd wanted to see what made Cecelia tick, sexually speaking.

Pale English men, with skinny legs apparently.

They hadn't even been holding hands and had stood as politely as two strangers while admiring an incredibly erotic work of art.

She'd jumped when she'd seen him, though! And blushed just a touch as she'd introduced Gordon to him.

And all the more Luka had wanted to know her in bed.

'Please,' he said now. 'Take a seat.'

Luka gestured to a chair and then went around his desk while Cecelia took her seat.

And then she faced him.

He really was a very beautiful man.

Aside from fancying him rotten and everything, Luka Kargas really was exquisite to look at.

Those velvet eyes awaited hers but she could not quite meet them and she took in the high cheekbones and full plump mouth.

Cecelia liked mouths.

Gordon's had been a bit small and pinched but she had only really thought that after she had seen Luka's.

No, she should never have taken the job in the first place.

The very second she'd entered his luxurious office and he had stood to greet her, Cecelia had known she should turn and run.

Until that point, she and Gordon had seemingly ticked

every box, yet that had changed the moment she'd shaken hands with Luka.

She had known that she *had* to end her engagement the night she had come back from the museum and while being intimate with Gordon had found herself imagining Luka instead.

It had been the best orgasm of her life!

Luka was everything that her aunt had warned her about.

Despite somehow knowing it could only end badly, and that she should leave now, instead she had taken the job.

And now she was here.

About to resign.

'There is something you wish to discuss?' Luka said, and she nodded.

It was all very formal and deliberately so, for Luka was not about to make this easy on her.

Quite simply he had never known a better PA and he did not want that to change.

He wanted Cecelia to stay and Luka *always* got what he wanted.

'So?' he invited. 'What is it that you have to say?'

It wasn't the first time she had handed in her notice and Cecelia was about to deliver her well-rehearsed lines yet she just sat there in strained silence. For when he held her gaze, as he did now, there felt like a limit on the oxygen in the vast room and superfluous words were rather hard to find.

'I'm leaving.'

'Pardon?' Luka checked, and cocked his head a little, as if he hadn't heard. He would make her say it again, and more explicitly this time.

'I shan't be renewing my contract.' After such an ap-

palling start the words now came tumbling out. 'I've
given it considerable thought and though it's been an
amazing year I've decided that it's time to move on.'

'But for all your *considerable thought*, you haven't
discussed it with me.'

'I don't need your permission to resign, Luka.'

Oh, this wasn't going well, Cecelia thought as she
heard the snap in her voice.

Yet she was almost at breaking point and that was
verified when Bridgette buzzed.

'There's a woman called Katiya down in Reception,
asking to see you, Luka...'

He rolled his eyes. 'I'm busy.'

'She's very insistent. Apparently you'll know why.'

'Tell Security that whoever lets her up will be fired.'

He looked over at Cecelia. 'Why can't women take
no for an answer?'

'Why can't my boss?'

'Touché,' he conceded and then decided to play the
sympathy card, 'Cecelia, *one* of the reasons I changed
my mind about taking the day off was that I have just
found out my mother is very unwell.'

'I'm sorry to hear that.' Cecelia said. 'If there's
any...' She stopped and then she closed her mouth rather
than continue.

'You were saying?' Luka checked, and when she
didn't respond he spoke for her. 'Because actually there
is something you can do for me. Cece, I am going to
be away a lot in the coming months. My mother has
cancer and will be undergoing extensive treatments...'

She felt her own rapid blink.

Luka never spoke of his family.

Ever!

'I am going to have to spend a lot of time in Xanero.

You're an amazing PA and I hope you know how much I appreciate you.' He saw the swallow in her throat and went in for the kill. 'At this difficult time, I don't want to deal with someone new.'

'Luka, I am sorry to hear that your mother is unwell but it doesn't sway my decision.'

She really was as cold as ice, and yet, and yet…as he looked across the desk he could see tension in her features and that those gorgeous green eyes could not meet his.

'Can I ask you to stay on for another six months? Naturally you'll be reimbursed…'

'Not everything is about money, Luka.'

He saw her green eyes flash and knew full well she thought him nothing more than a rich playboy.

She knew nothing about his start in life and Luka certainly wasn't about to enlighten her.

No one knew the truth.

Even his own parents seemed to believe the lie that had long been perpetuated—that the resort on Xanero Island and the original famous Kargas restaurant housed within it had given Luka his start in life.

Well, it hadn't.

Sex had.

Affluent holidaymakers looking for a thrill had first helped Luka to pave his way from near poverty to the golden lifestyle he had now.

The more sanitised PR version was that the first Kargas restaurant had given Luka his start.

Lies, all lies.

Not that he had any reason to tell Cecelia that.

Luka did not have to explain himself to his PA.

'What if I offered more annual leave?'

'I've already accepted another role.'

And so, when being nice and accommodating didn't work, Luka grew surly. 'With whom?'

'I don't need to answer that.'

'Actually, Cece—'

'Don't call me that!' she reared. 'Luka, on the one hand you tell me how much you appreciate the work I do and yet you can't even be bothered to get my name right.'

Finally he had his reaction.

'So you're leaving because I don't call you by your correct name?'

'No.'

'Then why?'

'I don't have to answer that.'

'Actually Ce-cel-i-a—' he drawled every syllable of her name '—if you look at your contract you cannot work for any of my rivals for a period of a year and you cannot—'

'Don't.' She halted him. 'Luka, I am allowed to leave.'

She was.

'Of course you are.' He just didn't like that fact.

'I've got four weeks left on my contract and naturally I'll start looking for my replacement straight away. Unless you have anyone particular in mind?'

'I'll leave all of that to you.'

'Sure.'

He flicked his hand in dismissal and Cecelia read the cue and headed out, though she did not return to her desk.

Once alone in the quiet of the bathrooms she leant against one of the cool marble walls.

She'd done it.

Possibly it was the worst career move she would ever make, but soon sanity would be restored to her mind.

No longer would she stand on a busy Tube in rush hour, wishing that somehow she was the woman lying beneath that depraved, beautiful face as he leaned in for a kiss...

No more would she have to breathe through her mouth when he was close just to avoid a hit of the heady scent of him.

Finally, the clenching low in her stomach at his lazy smile would dissipate.

Order would be restored to the chaos he had made of her heart.

Not yet, though.

It really was an awful day.

Flowers were delivered for Luka that Cecelia signed for, and then stupidly she read the card.

Oh, the offer from Katiya was very explicit.

And if he would just give her the elevator code then Katiya could come right up now, it would seem, and get straight on her knees.

Cecelia returned the card to the envelope and took them in to him.

'A delivery for you.'

'From?'

'I have no idea.'

He opened the card and then tossed it.

'Have them if you want,' he said, gesturing to the flowers.

'No, thank you.'

'Then put them somewhere that I can't see them.'

In case you get tempted? Cecelia wanted to ask.

But of course she didn't.

And then the downstairs receptionists messed up and a call was put through to Luka, but thankfully she was in his office at the time and it was Cecelia who answered it.

'I just need to speak to him…' a woman, presumably Katiya, sobbed.

'I'm sorry, Mr Kargas isn't taking any unscheduled calls,' Cecelia duly said.

Luka didn't even look up from his computer.

'What time do you have to finish today?' he asked when she ended the call.

'Any time,' Cecelia said, surprised by the unusual question, because Luka never usually bothered to ask. 'Why?'

'I want you to move the meeting with Garcia to the close of business there.'

'I'll see what I can do.'

'And I need you to sort out my flight tomorrow to Xanero. I'll be away for a couple of weeks.'

'A couple of weeks?' Cecelia checked, because for him to be away for that length of time was unheard of. Luka used his jet the way most people used public transport.

'I already told you,' Luka said and his voice was curt. 'My mother is ill.'

With his flight arranged, Luka rang Sophie Kargas and told her that her only child would be back tomorrow.

'One thing,' Luka said. 'I shan't be there to hold your hand and watch you give in. You're going to fight this.'

'Luka, I'm tired, I don't want any fuss. I just want you to come home.'

He could hear the defeat in her voice and he knew only too well the reason. The treatment would mean regular trips to Athens and Theo Kargas liked his wife to be at home.

Yes, it was a very long and difficult day spent avoiding each other as best they could but the tension hung heavy in the air at the office.

'I have your mother on the phone,' Cecelia said as afternoon gave way to evening.

'Tell her I'm in a meeting.'

'Of course.'

He really was a bastard, Cecelia decided as she relayed the message to the feeble-sounding woman.

'But I just need to speak with him for a moment.'

'I'm so sorry,' Cecelia said. 'Luka can't take any calls right now. I know he's busy trying to clear up as much of his schedule as he can today.'

Luka sat with his hands behind his head and his feet on the desk.

He could not face speaking to his mother again today and hearing how she had as good as given up on life.

Well, he would deal with all that tomorrow, for what Luka had to say would be better said face to face.

Leave him.

It wouldn't be the first time he had said it to his mother, but he hoped it would be the last.

Always he had hoped that his father would die first, if only to afford his mother some peace.

He glanced at the time and saw that it was approaching seven.

The meeting with Garcia was now scheduled for ten.

Luka got up and put on his jacket and then headed out of the office.

Cecelia didn't look up; instead she carried on tapping away on her computer, pretending she hadn't noticed him.

'Truce,' Luka said, and he saw her shoulders drop a little as her tense lips relaxed in a small smile.

'Truce,' Cecelia said, and she looked up at him.

'Let's go and get dinner.'

Her heart dropped.

Not that she showed it.

Cecelia wanted this day to be over.

More than anything she loathed going to dinner with him.

Or rather she loved going to dinner with him.

Luka was incredibly good company.

But that only made it all so much worse.

CHAPTER THREE

'I'LL JUST GO and freshen up,' Cecelia said and reached for her bag.

'Sure.'

He was lounging on her desk again and she had to step over his long legs to get past.

In the luxurious bathrooms of Kargas Holdings, Cecelia stared in the mirror and told herself that in four weeks this slow torture would be over.

She retied her hair and topped up her lipstick and, unable to help herself, checked her phone to see if her aunt—or anyone—had messaged her for her birthday.

No.

As disappointing as it was about her aunt and uncle, the real truth was that Cecelia could think of nothing nicer than going out for dinner with Luka on her birthday.

Except this wasn't a date—she was going out with her boss for a work dinner and Cecelia knew she would have to spend the next couple of hours constantly reminding herself of that fact.

When she came out, Luka was standing, waiting, and she felt his eyes on her as she retrieved her little bolero and put it on.

God, but he loathed it.

It was the colour of mustard and he'd far prefer to see her pale flesh. He would love to tell her just that, but with Cecelia he was constantly on his best behaviour.

'Ready?' he checked, and she nodded.

'Ready.'

His driver delivered them to a gorgeous Greek restaurant on the river that had recently opened.

'Time to check out the competition,' Luka said as they were led to a beautifully set table, but Luka refused it.

'We'll eat outside,' he said.

They were soon seated at a beautiful spot overlooking the river.

'The music would drive me crazy in there,' Luka told her, though the real reason was that they had the air-conditioning cranked up and he wanted her to be rid of that cardigan.

What the hell was wrong with him, Luka thought, that he would sit outside just for the thrill of seeing her upper arms.

Her arms!

'Here's perfect,' Cecelia said as she took her seat. 'There's a lovely breeze from the river.'

'Of course there is,' Luka said, but she didn't understand his wry smile.

It certainly wasn't the first time they had eaten together, although it wasn't often that they did. When they travelled, Cecelia had taken to having her breakfast sent to her hotel room as she could not bear to see him breakfasting with whomever he was seeing at the time.

Often, when away, she and Luka had lunch together but generally there were guests or clients involved.

As for dinner?

She had no idea, neither did she want to know what

Luka did by night and so, when away, and the working day had ended, she generally opted for room service.

Now she looked through the menu but could not concentrate for she was certain he would again try to dissuade her from leaving.

He didn't, though, and instead he selected the wine. 'What would you like?'

'Not for me.' Cecelia said.

'Of course not.' He rolled his eyes. Heaven forbid she relax in his company, but he asked for sparkling water.

She gave her order to the waiter, which, despite its fancy wording, was basically a tomato salad.

Luka ordered *bourdeto*.

She had seen it on the menu and read that it was made with scorpion.

Apt, for there would be a sting in his tail and she could feel it.

Oh, the surroundings were beautiful and the conversation polite but she could feel her own tension as she awaited attack. For Luka did not give in easily, that much she knew.

Life was a chessboard to him and every move was planned.

Now that his mother was ill, he had very good reasons to want an efficient PA, one capable of steering the helm while he was away.

Yes, she was braced, if not for attack then for the silk of his persuasion. But she must not relent, not now that she had finally had the courage to hand in her notice.

'A taste of home,' he said as their dishes were served.

'Will it be nice to be there?' Cecelia asked. 'Aside from the difficult news, I mean.'

Luka just shrugged.

'Will you be staying with your family?' she asked.

She wasn't probing, she told herself, for there were arrangements to be made that would undoubtedly fall to her.

'The resort is huge. They have a villa there but on the other side to mine.'

'What's it like in Xanero?'

'The island is stunning.'

'It's still a family business?' Cecelia checked.

'Yes.' It wasn't an outright lie but there was so much he left unsaid.

'Your father's still the chef there?'

Luka didn't answer straight away.

The truth was, his father had never been the chef there. Well, once, for the briefest of times.

It was all part of an elaborate charade that Luka went along with, only so that his mother could hold her head up in town.

'He's semi-retired,' Luka said, and that wasn't really a lie—Theo Kargas had spent his adult life semi-retired. Still, rather than talk about home he moved the subject to the upcoming weeks. Not everything had been cancelled. Luka would be working online and there was a trip to Athens he would keep. It was doable yet it was complex as Luka was booked out weeks and months ahead of time, so there was never much room for manoeuvre.

'I'll tell Garcia that the trip to New York will have to wait.'

'He won't like it.'

'Good,' Luka said. 'You know what they say about treating them mean to keep them keen. He needs me far more than I need him, yet he has started to forget that! Still, perhaps we can go when I return.'

'Of course.' Cecelia nodded. 'When you know more

how things are at home I'll schedule it again. Hopefully by then your new PA will be on board and he or she can go along too.'

He didn't like the sound of that.

Luka looked over to where she sat, sipping on sparking water with that mustard-coloured cardigan covering cream shoulders, and *still* he wondered what made her tick.

Cecelia intrigued him.

She was as cold as ice and so buttoned up and formal that, even though he knew she'd been engaged, he privately wondered if she was a virgin, for he simply could not imagine her in bed.

But on occasion he found himself imagining it anyway!

'What happened to Gordon?' Luka suddenly asked.

Her silence was a pointed one.

'Come on,' he said, 'you're leaving—I can ask now.'

'I like to keep my private life private,' Cecelia said, stabbing an olive with her fork.

'I know you do,' Luka said. 'Come on, what happened?'

Cecelia hesitated.

Certainly she would not be telling Luka that at inappropriate times images of him had kept popping into her head! And neither would she tell him that she had thought herself content until he'd appeared in her life.

Instead, she told him a far safer version. 'I decided that my aunt and uncle's version of the perfect man for me didn't fit mine.'

'Your aunt and uncle?' he checked, recalling that Cecelia's aunt was her next of kin on her résumé.

'I was raised by them after my mother died.'

'How old were you then?'

'Eight,' Cecelia said through taut lips, for she was terribly uncomfortable with the subject, but Luka seemed very intent on finding things out tonight.

'What about your father?'

She gave a slight shake of her head, which told him nothing other than the subject was out of bounds.

Not just with Luka.

She had never told anyone about the time she had come face to face with him.

He had dark hair and had worn a wedding ring.

That was all Cecelia knew. That and the fact he had shouted at her mother. When the money had run out, Harriet had called him to tell him he had a child, but it hadn't produced the result her mother had obviously hoped for.

There had been no joyful greeting. His eyes had been furious when they had met hers, and Harriet had quickly sent her daughter to her room.

A lot of shouting had ensued and Cecelia had found out that her mother had once been given a considerable sum of money for… Cecelia had frowned when she heard a word that a seven-year-old Cecelia didn't understand.

Termination.

Soon after, to her terrible distress, she found out what her father had meant.

'I don't want to talk about my father,' she said to Luka.

'Fine.' He shrugged and then gave that wicked smile. 'Tell me more about your fiancé, then.'

'Ex,' she pointed out.

'That's right.'

At the time, the only reason he had guessed her engagement was over had been the lack of a ring and the absence of his calls. There had been no tears from Cecelia or days off and no impact on her efficiency that he'd been able to see.

'Was it you who ended it?'

Cecelia gave a terse nod.

'How did he take it?'

'Luka!' she warned.

'I'm just curious. I've never been with anyone long enough to be engaged. I can't imagine getting that close to someone.' His eyes narrowed a little as he looked at her, still trying, as he had been since the day they had met, to gauge her. 'Was there someone else involved? Is that why you ended it?'

'Of course not,' she bristled.

'Did you live together?'

'I really don't want to discuss my private life,' Cecelia said. '*You* don't.'

'Yes, I do.'

'No, Luka, you don't. I might deal with your exes but I know nothing about you—'

'That's not true.'

'How long has your mother been ill?'

His jaw gritted and Cecelia gave a little smirk as she took a sip of her water.

'Fair enough.' He watched as she put down her glass and told her a truth. 'I'm going to miss *not* getting to know you, though.'

She would miss him far more than he knew.

'Is there anything I can do to dissuade you from leaving?' he asked.

She looked up at his voice for his tone had surprised her. She had expected sulky, or manipulative, or for more money to be waved in front of her.

Instead he *asked* if there was anything he could do to keep her.

'No.' Cecelia said, and then she cleared her throat, for the word had come out huskily. 'Luka, I will be here for another month and I will find the best replacement that I can. I'll train her myself. It really has been an amazing year but I'm ready for a new challenge.'

'So I'm no longer a challenge?'

'Of course you are,' Cecelia said.

He was actually a constant challenge to her senses— recklessness crept in whenever he was near, which Cecelia had to fight constantly just to keep it in check.

'How was the *bourdeto*?' Cecelia asked as his plate was removed unfinished.

Luka shrugged.

He had far more on his mind than food.

'What if I promise to stop calling you Cece?' he suggested. 'It takes twenty-one days to form a habit.'

'It actually takes sixty-six days,' Cecelia corrected. 'So there isn't time for that. But thanks for offering.' And then she smiled, something Cecelia so rarely did.

Rather, she rarely smiled *properly*, but now, as she did so, Luka watched as she checked herself midway and it dimmed.

For Luka, the fading of her smile felt like summer was ending.

It was, of course.

In a few weeks' time summer would be gone.

Of course it would come around again, but this summer, *this* one, would never return.

'Was Gordon upset when you finished with him?' Luka asked. 'And before you tell me that it's private, I know it is.'

'So why ask now?'

'Because you're the best PA I've ever had, and I didn't want to push you into leaving by getting too personal, but now that you've already resigned I don't have to behave.'

'Yes, you do,' Cecelia said, and though her voice remained even there was a flurry of nerves low in her stomach as to what her boldness today had unleashed.

So she answered the question.

'Yes, he was upset, although, to be honest, I think he was more embarrassed than upset.'

'No, I imagine he was very upset,' Luka said in his deep, low voice, and met her eyes. Suddenly the cool breeze from the river felt like a warm one.

At times, Luka would disregard her professional boundaries and flirt with her.

Like now.

That little hint of his silken charm carried from his lips and sent a slow shiver the length of Cecelia's spine.

'I'd better get back to the office,' Cecelia said, 'and set up for your meeting.'

But he would prefer to linger.

The changing world was waiting and it was nice to be here by the river.

With her.

'Garcia can wait,' Luka said.

'One day he might get tired of waiting.'

'I doubt it,' Luka said. 'Right now he wants to wrap up the purchase.'

'I thought you wanted a hotel in New York City.'

'I do,' Luka said, 'but at a price of my choosing. Anyway, we need to talk about your replacement.'

'I've informed the agency you generally use,' Cecelia said, and Luka frowned.

'You weren't referred via them?'

'No.' Cecelia shook her head.

'Ah, that's right, you were working for Justin. How did you end up with him?'

'Via the agency,' Cecelia said, and she itched to get back and away from his gaze but Luka wasn't letting her go just yet.

'How did you become a PA?'

More questions, Cecelia thought, but this wasn't such a personal one and so she was a little freer in her response. 'I never intended to be. When I finished school I had wanted to travel,' she told him, 'or go to university, but...' Cecelia hesitated. 'My uncle had a friend who needed a nanny in France. I spoke French—well, a little—and he said that way I'd get to travel and work at the same time.'

'The trust fund ran out, you mean.'

'Sorry?' Cecelia blinked.

'They would have received money to raise you, but once you turned eighteen—'

'No,' Cecelia interrupted. 'It wasn't like that at all.' She shook her head. 'They were very good to take me in.'

'Did they have children?'

'No,' Cecelia said, and she swallowed because she believed they had very much been childless by choice.

Luka's comments needled for she had always felt rather in the way with her aunt and uncle, not that she'd admit it to him. 'My uncle had a contact who needed a nanny.'

'Really, Cece! You? A nanny?'

He could not imagine the very crisp and proper Cecelia working with children and he actually smiled at the very thought, parting those gorgeous lips to show his pearly white teeth.

Gosh, he had such a nice mouth.

'I hated it,' Cecelia admitted. 'I lasted four weeks before I gave notice, but then the mother, a television producer, asked if I could work for her instead. I guess it all started from there.'

'Do you still see your aunt and uncle?'

'Of course,' Cecelia said confidently, although inside she wavered for it had always been her making the effort rather than them.

They hadn't so much as sent a text for her birthday.

Perhaps a card would have arrived in the mail when she got home.

Or there would be flowers on her doorstep.

Yet she knew there wouldn't be.

Her birthday had passed by unnoticed again and it hurt.

She would not let Luka see it, of course, but his comment about the trust-fund money drying up had perturbed her.

'Do you want dessert?' he asked, knowing the answer.

'No, thank you.'

'Tough,' Luka said. 'You're getting one.'

She went to ask what he meant but at that moment the background music wafting out of the restaurant changed to a very familiar tune and she turned as she saw a waiter with a slice of cake and atop it a candle.

The tune was 'Happy Birthday'!

And it was being played for her.

'Luka…'

Cecelia was embarrassed.

Pleased.

And utterly caught by surprise.

No one remembered her birthday.

Ever.

As a child, it had fallen in the school holidays and her mother had only liked grown-up parties, certainly not the type Cecelia had dreamed of. And after she had died, Cecelia hadn't readily made friends. In fact, at boarding school she had been endlessly teased and bullied.

At eighteen, her aunt and uncle had given up on the perfunctory birthday card and last-minute present, which had always, *always* been something she needed rather than something she might want.

This was the first time that she'd truly been spoiled on her birthday.

There were two spoons and the cake was completely delectable—vanilla sponge drizzled in thick lemon syrup that was both tart and refreshing.

And she was sharing dessert on her birthday with him.

Luka Kargas.

Cecelia was almost scared to look up for she was worried there might be tears in her eyes.

'Here,' Luka said, 'is the other reason I came into the office today.'

Now Cecelia did look up as he went into his jacket and pulled out a gorgeous parcel and slid it across the table.

It was a long box wrapped in deep red velvet and tied with ribbon that had a little gold charm attached to it.

And she frowned because Cecelia recognised the packaging.

On one overseas trip, she had enjoyed staring into the window of a lavish boutique in the foyer of a Florence hotel where they had been staying. Whenever she'd been waiting for Luka, she had indulged herself with the joy of admiring the beautiful jewellery.

She pulled back the bow, but first she had a question for she didn't quite believe what Luka had said. 'You didn't really come in just because it's my birthday?'

'Of course I did. I always try to do the right thing on my PA's birthday.'

Luka knew full well that for Cecelia he had done more than just the right thing. Usually it was flowers and perfume, or a voucher for a spa hotel, but a few weeks ago, on a business trip, he had stepped out of the elevator and Cecelia's back had been to him. He had looked to where her gaze had been focused and spied the sparkling window display of the hotel boutique.

The next morning she had been looking again.

And the next.

It had sat in his bureau at home for weeks now.

Last night, just after he had fired off the text to say that he wouldn't be in, he had remembered her birthday.

Luka had been partying hard, trying to forget the news that had come in about his mother, trying to extend the weekend into a long one, just to delay the return home.

And then he had remembered the box inside his bureau.

'Oh!' She gave a gasp of recognition when she saw the necklace. 'How on earth…?' It was thick and lavish, coiled with rubies, or glass, she wasn't sure—Cecelia hadn't even asked the price at the time, for in either case it would have been way out of her league; she had simply adored it, that was all. 'Luka, it's far too much.'

'It can double up as your leaving gift,' Luka brooded. 'Do you want to put it on?'

'No,' she said too quickly, 'I'll wait till I'm home.'

She wouldn't be able to manage the clasp and she

would burst into flames at the touch of his hands if he so much as brushed the sensitive skin of her neck.

The breeze from the river wasn't helping at all now. The tiny cardigan felt like a thick shawl around her shoulders and she simply didn't know how to react.

'How did you even know it was my birthday?' Cecelia asked, because she hadn't mentioned it and certainly she hadn't made a note of it in his diary.

'I make it my business to know.' He could see she was shaken and her reaction surprised him. He had thought she'd be more than used to a fuss being made but she actually seemed stunned, even close to tears. 'I fired a PA once, about ten years ago,' he explained as a waiter put down two small glasses, a bottle of ouzo and a carafe of iced water on the table between them.

'No, thank you,' Cecelia said as he went to pour one for her. 'You were saying.'

Luka went ahead and added iced water to the ouzo and she watched as the clear liquid turned white.

How she would love to try it, but she had to keep her guard up, for it was becomingly increasingly difficult to remember that this was work.

He did this for all his PAs, Cecelia reminded herself, and forced herself to listen rather than daydream as he told her just why he had made such a nice fuss.

'As I was firing her she started to cry.'

'Tears don't usually trouble you,' Cecelia said, thinking of the many tears women had shed over him.

'They don't,' Luka said, 'but as she was clearing out her things she said that it was her worst birthday ever. She was a terrible PA and deserved to be fired, but I didn't set out to ruin her birthday.'

'You really felt bad?' Cecelia checked, pleased that he did have a conscience after all.

'A bit,' he agreed. 'Since then I have tried to keep track. Normally I would have taken you for lunch. In fact, that was what I had planned to do but when it came to it I was sulking too much to do so...'

She smiled again and back came summer.

'I thought, given it's your birthday, that you would have plans tonight. That's why I checked what time you had to leave by.'

'No, no plans.'

It was her best birthday ever.

Luka couldn't know that, of course, but even Gordon hadn't made much of a fuss.

They'd gone for dinner.

But there had been no candles and no cake.

Gordon had bought her a cloying perfume Cecelia hadn't liked.

It wasn't so much the lavishness of the gift Luka had given her that made it the best, more the thought behind it.

How he had seen her looking at the necklace.

That he had noticed...

Yes, she was right to leave.

Because of this.

Because of those moments when he put her world to rights and she was utterly and completely crazy about him.

She had grown up with the dour warning that she did not want to end up like her mother and that men like Luka could only lead her down a dangerous path.

Yet, to her shame, it beckoned her at times.

Times like tonight.

When the easiest thing in the world would be to thank him with a kiss.

She knew where it would lead, though, for that was exactly where she wanted it to lead.

And Luka wouldn't be hard to convince!

He was easy.

That much she knew.

He was, though, at least with her, the perfect gentleman.

Well, not perfect, and not always a gentleman, but from the beginning Luka had, in the main, accepted her boundaries and there had been no overt flirting.

Occasionally he would slip, but he'd quickly rein it in. He wasn't a sleaze and played only where welcome. More than that, though, his world worked far better with Cecelia in it. He recognised talent and certainly she was brilliant at her job. Luka knew full well that he would lose the best PA he'd ever had if he chased that perpetual want.

And there was want in him.

Yet he knew his own track record, and Luka had never lasted with anyone for more than a month.

But look where behaving had got him, Luka thought.

He'd lost her anyway.

He decided now was the time to find out more about her.

'How did your mother die?' Luka asked, though he had already guessed her response—*That's personal, Luka*, or, *That's not your concern.*

She was about to deliver a response just like that, but then she remembered she was leaving.

Perfection was no longer required now that she had resigned.

And so she told him the truth, or at least the little she knew of it.

'I believe she took too much cocaine.'

CHAPTER FOUR

OH, CECELIA!

Luka hadn't expected to find out much at all, let alone that her mother had died from a cocaine overdose.

He thought of her, so prim and controlled, and had assumed her upbringing had caused that. Well, he concluded, it *had*, but not in the way he had imagined.

Still, he said nothing, because he didn't want to say the wrong thing, and he desperately wanted to hear more.

Cecelia liked his patient silence. There wasn't so much as a flicker of reaction that she could read in his expression as she revealed the dark truth, and Cecelia inwardly thanked him for that. 'She was at a party, I've been told.'

'Was it a one-off—?' he started to ask, but Cecelia cut in.

'No, it was a regular occurrence. My mother loved to party, she lived a very debauched life.'

'And you lived with her?'

'I did.' Cecelia nodded.

'What was that like?'

She wanted warm memories of her early childhood.

Cecelia wanted to say that in spite of everything there had been so many amazing times and that despite her mother's ways she'd been loved.

Yet she could not, and so she described what it had been like to live with her mother. 'Unsafe.'

Yes, he understood her a little better now.

He thought of her neat desk and tidy drawers and her utter reluctance to unbend and have fun, but now he watched as she reached for her purse and stood.

'We had better get back,' Cecelia told him, deciding that she had said far too much.

'No, sit,' Luka said, but she shook her head.

'I don't have time to sit by the river and reminisce,' Cecelia said. 'And neither do you. You have a meeting with Garcia at ten.'

'I've already said he can wait.'

Well, she wouldn't.

Cecelia walked off swiftly, embarrassed and unsure why she had told him about her mother when usually she did all she could to conceal that side of her past.

Usually she loathed people's reactions to it—their shocked expressions and the recriminations. She felt like crying as she remembered her so-called friends' reactions at boarding school when they had stumbled on the salacious news articles and the endless dissection of her mother's death.

Schooldays had certainly not been the best times of Cecelia's life.

They had read out every embarrassing detail to each other with relish as she had lain in her bed in the dorm, night after night. And then had come the endless questions.

'Was it a party or an orgy your mother was at?' Lucy, the ringleader had asked. *'And what do they mean by "compromising position"?'*

It hadn't been much better during term breaks. Cecelia's pace quickened as she thought of her aunt and uncle. They had rarely mentioned her mother and when they had they'd spoken in disapproving tones.

The deeper truth was that home had been no better, because actually her aunt and uncle had rarely spoken to her at all.

As for Gordon—well, with him, her mother had been *she who must not be named*, just a sordid part of Cecelia's past that was best forgotten.

Yet Luka had wanted to know more about it.

'Wait,' he called, and though she did not slow down he soon caught up with her. 'Why walk off when we're talking?'

'Because there's work to do, because…' *You're work.*

Constantly she had to remind herself of that fact.

Four more weeks of this felt too long, but then Cecelia reminded herself that he would be away for the next two.

She would be mad to get involved with him.

Mad.

She wasn't flattering herself to believe she could have him.

Cecelia also knew Luka well enough to know it would only be for a night, or a couple of weeks at best.

Cecelia knew, absolutely, how it would end—indifference, then avoidance—for she had seen it all too many times, and the trouble was that she did not know how she would recover.

She had never felt such *violent* emotions about someone before.

Luka Kargas was her one weakness and that would never do.

And so, after their gorgeous riverside dinner, they took the elevator back up in silence. Back in the office, she went to set up for the meeting that had been rescheduled and delayed over and over again. She made sure his notes were on his desk and she tried to ignore the rich scent of him as she chatted online with Stacey, who was Mr Garcia's PA.

'He's going to be another half-hour,' Stacey said, and Cecelia inwardly groaned for she just wanted this day to be over with. 'Are you able—?' Her voice cut off and the screen went black, and only then did Cecelia register that Luka had deliberately turned the computer off.

'What on earth are you doing?' she asked.

'I don't like to be kept waiting.'

'But you were the one who cancelled this morning's meeting.'

'So...' Luka shrugged '...tomorrow you can say that we lost the connection. I can't sit through a meeting about figures now.'

'Fine,' Cecelia snapped.

This bloody meeting had been moved and delayed so many times that she wondered how anyone did business with him.

Yet she knew the answer.

Luka was brilliant.

And they would wait.

'I want to talk to you,' Luka said.

'Is it about work?' Cecelia asked.

'No.'

'Then there's nothing to discuss. I'll go and pack for you,' Cecelia said. 'And then I'll be off.'

She headed to his suite.

Usually it took five minutes to pack for him as she had it down pat, but he wasn't going away for business and his wardrobe here consisted mainly of suits, shirts and ties.

She stood in his suite looking at his wardrobe for a moment as if more choices might appear, and then headed out.

He was sitting on her desk, as he had been this morning, only she chose not to sit down this time.

'I don't know what to pack,' she admitted. 'Are you staying here tonight?'

Luka nodded.

'Then I can go to your apartment and select a more casual wardrobe. I'll bring your luggage in with me in the morning.'

'Sure.'

She picked up her bag and gave him a tight smile. 'Thank you for dinner and cake and my gorgeous present.'

'You're most welcome.'

His dark eyes met hers and she wondered if she should give him a kiss on the cheek to thank him, just as she would anyone else who had given her such a nice night and gift.

Only he was not anyone.

But tonight of all nights, her hard-won control slipped and she leant in and gave him a light kiss on the cheek.

She merely brushed the skin of his cheek with her lips, and she even held her breath to lessen the impact the gesture would have on her senses. She would taste him later; in the elevator she would run her tongue over her lips and recall the warmth of his skin on her mouth.

And she would recall too the ache in her breast at the mere graze against his shirt.

She pulled back and her bag bit into her shoulder as she ached to drop it to the floor and give in to her craving for this man.

Luka did not want to get this wrong.

He read women with ease, and his kiss was so rarely refused—yet with her he could not be certain.

She had chastised him with her eyes on so many occasions, he could almost feel the sting of the slap she would deliver if he put so much as a finger wrong.

It would be worth it, Luka decided.

'I'll see you tomorrow,' Cecelia said, her voice a touch high as she willed her legs to move and take her from danger.

Yet, and yet… 'But if you need anything before that…'

She had said the same words a hundred times before—or was it a thousand times?—but they sounded different tonight.

His response was different tonight too. 'I need to be with you.'

No slap was delivered, she just stared back. And right when she thought she might finally know his kiss, instead his hands came to her arms.

'Aren't you going to try it on?'

She thought again of those slender dark fingers in her hair and his mouth near her cheek as he did the clasp, only this time, instead of refusing, she nodded.

'Let me help,' Luka said. He took her bag from her shoulder and retrieved the present and then dropped the bag to the floor.

He slowly prised open the box and as she watched his long finger run over the stones and she felt as if he was stroking her on the inside.

Luka could hear the trip in her breathing and felt the charge in the air; he breathed in the scent of seduction. For that was what she did, Luka concluded—without so much as a word or a move, she seduced.

'Turn around,' Luka said, and he moved from lounging against her desk.

Cecelia did so.

At his simple command she turned and faced the wall.

She had known how this evening would end, how this year would end.

And they ended tonight, she was suddenly rather certain of that.

But it didn't matter now.

She was leaving.

Cecelia went to lift the long ponytail she had retied many times today, but he pushed her hand down. 'I've got this,' Luka said.

She could barely breathe as she felt his hands come around her throat and the brush of his fingers against the pulse in her neck. He was tall and, she was certain, hard behind her, and she ached to lean back into him.

She felt the coolness of the necklace fall between her breasts as he put it on and the brush of his fingers as he did up the clasp. But then, instead of turning her around to admire the necklace, his fingers moved to the tiny bolero. She both heard and felt his voice. 'I hate this,' he said, and his words reverberated deep within her as he pushed the fabric down over her shoulders.

Luka would not rush this, for he had waited a long time and so first he removed the little bolero that he had loathed on sight.

One arm was freed, and then the other, and as the garment fell silently to the floor, she felt it dust her calf.

She shivered as he ran fingers along the bare flesh of her arms, something he had wanted to do all night.

'Luka…' His name from her lips was so loaded with lust that he did not take it as a reproach. Instead, he lifted her hair and the spine that had teased him this morning was now his to explore.

She felt his lips on the back of her neck as soft as the kiss she had delivered to his cheek and the message was the same, for it felt like a promise.

Every notch to her spine that was exposed by her dress was rewarded with a graze of his mouth, and then there was the ache of no contact for a moment.

Followed by delicious relief.

'I want to see this necklace on you as it should be seen,' he said. She felt his hands on her neck as he undid the tie of her halter neck and she bit her lip as he undid her flesh-coloured strapless bra.

Her breasts felt heavy and there was a yearning for his touch there, but instead he freed her hair and arranged it over her shoulders. For a second, just a second, his fingers grazed her breasts.

He felt her hard nipples, and now it was his breathing that was jagged for the longing to see her was intense. But their first kiss would be a naked one, Luka decided.

Cecelia could barely stand. She heard a noise and glanced to the side, seeing Luka toss his jacket over a chair. She turned back to face the wall, not sure whether she could bear to watch him undress.

And then she heard him strip off his shirt and she almost folded over at the thought of his naked chest behind her.

Her thighs were trembling and she would have no choice but to ask to sit soon, but then came his hands on her shoulders and another command. 'Turn around.'

Now she faced him and he looked at her usually pale face all flushed as if she'd already come. But instead of reproach in her green eyes there was the beckoning of an aurora as they glittered with the promise of what was to come.

'It's looks beautiful.'

The necklace fell between her breasts yet, as fine as it was, it garnered only a glance because he had found perfection elsewhere. He experienced a fierce desire to taste her there and to explore with his fingers, though they had not yet so much as kissed.

His lips were warm as they brushed over hers. Her breasts got the tease of his naked skin as their bodies came together, then his arms pulled her in as she moaned at the contact. He tasted of anise and all things forbidden and delicious.

And then he kissed her hard and she kissed him back hungrily, for she had craved him for close to a year. Her hands slipped through the arms that held her and came up behind his head to pull him closer.

He had expected reticence, that her tongue would require his coaxing, yet instead together they fuelled urgent desire. The woman who rarely blushed, who was always so cool and distant now burnt at his touch. He had imagined a slow seduction perhaps, and then he laughed in his head that he had thought her a virgin for the woman in his arms was wanton and wild.

He pressed against her hips and her grip tightened in his hair.

Tiny nips and wet, hot kisses were shared as Luka pressed her to the wall. She was grateful for the support it gave as her legs were trembling.

Luka pressed into her and moved her hands from his head and down past his flat stomach to the hard heat that was pressed into her.

He pulled back and their foreheads met as they watched her free him.

And, because it was Luka, of course he had protection to hand. But before he was lost to latex, Cecelia held him for a moment, as she had so long wanted to—stroking his thick, hard length as beads of silver moistened her palm.

She licked her lips and he moaned a low curse, for he wanted to carry her now to his suite. Luka wanted the rest of Cecelia's clothes to be gone, but his want was more immediate now. He pushed her hand away and sheathed himself with rapid, practised ease and then got back to her mouth.

He was so tall that even with Cecelia in high espadrilles she was no match for him.

Their teeth clashed and suddenly too much was not enough. He pushed up the dress and his hands roughly roamed her inner thighs and felt her hot and wet as he tore at her knickers and then crouched enough to sear into her.

He was rougher than she had ever known yet there was liquid silk to ease his path.

Cecelia had never been more frantic and as he lifted her legs she wrapped them around him. He was strong enough with his grip to allow her to hold his face and kiss him back hard.

It was the roughest and most delicious coupling.

For they matched.

His hands held her buttocks and his fingers dug in so deep that they would surely leave a bruise, yet she ground onto him. And far from reticence, it was Cecelia coaxing him to come. 'Luka!' She could not focus on kissing, and she tore her mouth away. He could feel the tease of intimate muscles and he thrust in hard and then swelled to the tight grip of her orgasm and her sensual sob called him to deliver deep.

Luka did, shuddering his release deep into her to the last twitches of hers.

And that part had her dizzy. The moan of him carried

without breath to her ears, and the sensual slide of their hot, damp bodies as they slowly brought themselves back from the far reaches of the divine space they had been in together. Kissing again, with languorous relish as the world faded in.

He lowered her down and she could feel the thump, thump of his heart against the flutter of hers. Cecelia rested her head on his shoulder and she was herself for the first time.

And herself was more reckless than she had ever dared to be.

'Come on.' He was tidying up, picking up discarded clothes, ready to be headed for his suite and to bed, to resume proceedings, this time at a more leisurely pace.

But she would not be waking up there, Cecelia decided.

One taste of heaven was more than enough and she had always sworn to leave before he dictated terms.

'I need to get home.'

She picked up her bra, but since it would be almost impossible to do it up she pushed it into her bag.

'Cece…' he said, and she didn't correct him, but she did pick up her shredded knickers and added them to her bag, and then with rather unsteady hands did up her halter neck.

'I really do need to get home, Luka.'

'You're not just running off.'

'I'm not running,' she corrected. 'I just want to go home.'

Her voice was incredibly composed. He looked at the necklace, heavy between gently curving breasts and the gorgeous flush of her climax.

But aside from throwing her over his shoulder, or

dragging her, it would seem that he couldn't stop her from leaving. She had made up her mind.

Usually it would be perfect.

A good orgasm, and then the absence of conversation—except there was more to her that he wanted to explore, and he was rather sure that there was more to come for *them*.

But she was checking herself in a small mirror compact, as she often did before she headed out.

'Thanks for an amazing night,' Cecelia said, and then, just as she had done previously, she leant forward and gave him a kiss on the cheek, as if the past half an hour had not taken place.

'Don't go home yet,' Luka said.

'I want to, though.'

And he couldn't really argue with that.

He watched as she walked to the elevator and pressed the button.

Cecelia stepped in and pressed for the lobby, unable to stop herself leaning against the cool mirrors, not really surprised by what had taken place.

She had wanted him so badly for months.

A man in a suit got in at the fourteenth floor and another at the seventh.

Cecelia nodded and smiled and then stared ahead as they inched down to the ground floor where she stepped out and walked across the foyer.

The cleaners had their buffers out and were polishing the marble floors.

Cecelia said goodnight to the doorman and stepped out into the night, but there was no cool breeze to greet her.

It was a sultry London night, but as she headed for the underground station she heard her name—'Ms Andrews?'

She turned around and saw that it was Luka's driver.

'Mr Kargas said you worked too late to take the underground.'

And of all the experiences of this night, this was the part she both hated and loved the most.

Loved that she was being taken care of by Luka, that he had thought to see her safely home.

Hated because by his very nature it was a mere temporary, tantalising glimpse of his world.

CHAPTER FIVE

CECELIA WAS TEMPTED to call in sick, but then that would suggest she regretted last night, which she didn't.

Instead, she regretted how she felt this morning, because rather than getting up to her alarm and facing the very early start to her day, Cecelia had brought a coffee to bed and sat in it looking at the necklace that Luka had given her.

Cecelia did not want to be one of those women who dared to hope that with her things might be different.

She just had to get through this morning and then she would have a bit of a reprieve in the next two weeks, and then hopefully by the time he came back from Xanero, normal services could be resumed.

For the first time, she hadn't put out her clothes the night before but Cecelia forgave herself that lapse.

She dressed in the navy suit that she should have worn yesterday and after checking her appearance left the flat. It was too early even for Mrs Dawson to be up and about as she left and took the Tube, not to the office but to Luka's apartment, to which she had keys.

The trouble with being a PA, especially to someone as successful as Luka, was that for the term of your contract you had access to their life in a way few did.

And, Cecelia had learned, if you happened to be crazy about the boss, it was a form of slow torture.

The doorman knew her and greeted her with a smile. She headed up in the elevator and then rang the bell and waited a moment before letting herself in.

Once, thinking he was still overseas, she had let herself in unannounced, without ringing the bell, and had found Luka in bed.

Neither alone nor sleeping.

Yes, working for Luka really was torture.

Cecelia walked in through the entrance hallway, but instead of heading to his bedroom she went through to the lounge and looked out over the view of Hyde Park, wondering how he would behave with her this morning in the office.

Would he carry on like it hadn't even happened, or would he expect her to be available to him as she served out her notice?

She gave a little shake of her head to clear such thoughts and wheeled the case she had brought with her towards the main bedroom.

Damn!

He was in bed, though thankfully this time alone.

And asleep.

It wasn't unusual to have to tiptoe around him, only this morning it was made more difficult, knowing she could have awoken next to him.

As quietly as she could, Cecelia opened up a wardrobe and, as the light inside came on, Cecelia heard him stir.

'Hey,' Luka said, his voice thick and sleepy.

'I'm just sorting out your luggage for your trip.'

And then he must have recalled what they had done the previous night because he asked, 'Why did you leave so abruptly?'

'Because I wanted to get home,' Cecelia said, and then she turned and gave him a small smile and did her best to keep it light. 'And I also wanted some sleep.'

'Yes, well, you wouldn't have got that had you stayed.' He put his hands behind his head and watched her pulling out a couple of casual shirts and adding them to the case.

'Will you be swimming when you're there?' she asked.

'What do you think, Cece?' he said.

It really had been a stupid question, given where he was headed, but it had been more to change the subject than to find out the answer.

'I think you should call me by my proper name,' she added, ignoring his question. Of course he would be swimming.

'It's not a holiday camp.' He grinned from the bed. 'The villas all have their own private pools,' Luka said as she headed into his en suite bathroom, then he let out a fond laugh of recall. 'Though there used to be just one main one. I used to work it.'

'Work it?' Cecelia laughed and called out from the en suite where she was collecting his cologne and things. 'Were you a cabana boy?'

'Yes.'

'Really?' She came to the door smiling, her hands full of toiletries. 'I was actually joking.'

'It's true, though. I used to head down there after school or during the holidays. It wasn't as luxurious then as it is now. There was a different owner then—Geo.'

'What was he like?'

'Lazy and a gambler,' Luka said, and he looked at her standing in the doorway and thought of all she had told him last night.

And all she had not.

There was a lot he hadn't told her either. He thought of her little jab yesterday about not everything being about money. She thought he'd had it all handed to him on a plate.

Everyone did.

He would have two weeks solid of it now; his father swanning around as if he had rebuilt the stunning complex from scratch, and—one thing that really annoyed Luka—complaining about the food when he feasted at the restaurant. Theo would sit there loudly stating that he made it better himself, when in truth Theo Kargas could not make his own coffee, let alone run a high-end kitchen.

Luka rather guessed that the uptight Cecelia might not be a forgiving audience for the story of his beginnings, and not the first person he would choose to share it with.

Luka wasn't used to sharing anything.

In business and in private he chose to take rather than to give.

Yet she had told him so much last night and the guilt of his past gnawed at his gut like a cancer—not that he would ever admit it.

'I would pick up the towels and get drinks and things. Then, when I finished school I got a job in Reception.'

Cecelia zipped up his toiletry bag and put it in his case and was just about to ask him about footwear when he said something that made her frown.

'Of course, I still *worked* the pool but it was in my own time and it wasn't towels that I was picking up.'

She looked up and met his eyes. 'Meaning?'

'Because I worked in Reception, I knew who the

richest women were because they had private access to the beach and the ocean view.'

'I'm not with you...'

'I think you are, Cece.'

She added a belt to his case and did not look at him but he could see two pink spots on her cheek.

In fact, she was embarrassed, wondering if it was because of the fact that sex was constantly on her mind around Luka that she was misinterpreting things.

'I made a lot of money, and I saved all of it. I made enough that when Geo lost a small fortune and was desperate for cash, I put in an offer for the restaurant and it was accepted.'

'You bought the restaurant?'

'Yes,' Luka said. 'I bought it and gave my father a share, so he might finally work in his own restaurant, as he had always said he wanted to do. Growing up, we had no money and he said there were no jobs but there *were* jobs. Pot-washing jobs but, still, it was work. He got really angry...' Luka didn't add that he'd got the worst beating of his life that night. 'My mother said he was a chef and that washing pots was beneath him. So, when I had the money, I bought him a share in a restaurant, one with the Kargas name on the door.'

'But how on earth did a pool boy get the money to buy a restaurant?'

'It wasn't the establishment it is now,' Luka pointed out.

'But even so! Are you saying you were a gigolo?'

'If you choose to call it that then, yes, I was,' Luka said, expecting her to snap his case closed and walk away.

Yet she didn't.

'But how?' Cecelia asked. 'I mean, how does it work?'

Luka shrugged. 'A smile, a nod. Often they would buy me a drink.'

'I thought it would be the other way around.'

'No.'

'And did you name a price?'

'Of course not,' Luka said. 'That would be in poor taste.'

'But how?' she asked, intensely curious. 'I mean, I just can't imagine…'

'What?' he said. 'You can't imagine naming your wants?'

'No!' Cecelia admitted. 'I can't.'

'Perhaps you should try it before you knock it!'

'No, thank you,' she said primly. 'And I can't imagine giving the cabana boy a wink and a nod.'

Luka smiled. 'The first time it happened was a surprise. I got chatting to one of the guests. She was a widow. I didn't really know her but she asked me to join her for dinner. I said no, Geo would not like me dining with the guests. She said we would dine in her suite then. And so I went up and we ate and then we…' He smiled. 'I'm sure you can guess the rest.'

'But I can't,' Cecelia said, for she wanted to know more, and in her curiosity she found herself sitting down on the bed. 'How old was she?'

'A good bit older than I was then. In her thirties, I think,' Luka said. 'She was my first.' He looked at her. 'Who was yours?'

'I don't have to answer that.'

'If you want to know more you do.'

'Gordon.'

He wrinkled his nose and Luka was surprised as something that felt like it should be called jealousy surged in his chest.

Which was ridiculous when he was telling her about his own depraved past.

'Well, my first was actually stunning—a divorcée. She was there with friends but had her own villa. I was there every night until morning and I thought I had found the keys to heaven. The morning she left she came into Reception and when Geo wasn't looking she gave me an envelope. I thought it was a letter. When I opened it there was a whole load of cash. Until that point I had thought it was a romance.'

'Were you hurt when she paid you?'

'Hell no,' he said. 'To tell the truth I was already starting to get restless.'

Cecelia suppressed an eye-roll and refrained from saying that perhaps it was an indicator of things to come, as Luka spoke on.

'I was trying to work out how to break it off but had decided to do so after her holiday. I was the naïve one back then.'

Cecelia gave a wry smile at that. 'I doubt you were ever naïve. And after she'd gone there was another?'

'Of course, although it wasn't always cash. Sometimes they would take me shopping for a watch or such like. Once a car...'

'A car?'

She started to laugh. An embarrassed laugh, but she was also very curious. 'Luka!'

'What?' He shrugged. 'I was always careful and it wasn't all sex.'

'What else?'

'Romance. Dinner. Shopping. But mainly talking.'

'You mean, saying what they wanted to hear?'

'Yep.'

'Did you care for them?'

'Some I did,' Luka said. 'Mostly it was work.' He met her eyes. 'They didn't all care for me, Cece. They paid for the full Luka Kargas treatment.'

For a few years the pool had been his playground and the pickings had always been rich.

'Anyway,' he said, 'once I had bought the restaurant I hired a decent chef and changed the décor.'

'What about your father?'

Luka didn't answer directly.

It felt disloyal to his mother to admit that his father hadn't so much as lifted a saucepan.

'The restaurant started to do well and was too busy for one chef. Though it didn't do *too* well—I made sure of that.'

'Why?'

'Because I knew it wouldn't be long until Geo blew things again and would be forced to sell. When that happened I had planned to be in a good enough position to put in an offer on the resort. With help, of course...'

'Financial help?' Cecelia checked.

'No, one of the women I was seeing helped me get my papers in order to go to the bank.' He didn't add that the woman had also warned him not to bring his father into the hotel side of things.

It was advice for which he would be grateful for ever.

'How old were you by then?'

'Twenty-two. Once the resort was safely mine I hired the best chef I could find and things really started to happen. As the guests came in I started to buy up the houses and land around it. Out of all the hotels I own, it is still the jewel in my crown. From humble beginnings it's magnificent now.'

She looked at him. He mesmerised her, he truly did.

And she was nervous too, for the more she knew him, the more she wanted him.

'Is your father still your business partner?'

'Not fully.' He shook his head. 'The hotels are mine, the restaurants belong to us both.' And then, a touch unguarded, he admitted a little more. 'I should never have gone into business with him.'

'I agree about not going into business with family,' Cecelia said, because she had seen such things go wrong in her work before. 'And, Luka, I also think it's a really bad idea getting involved with an employer.' It was Cecelia who brought it back to them. 'I'm not saying that I regret last night, but it should never have happened. I take my career very seriously.'

'I know you do, but you're leaving anyway.'

'Yes,' she agreed. 'But I still don't think it's right and I don't want Bridgette or anyone knowing that something once happened between us.'

'Once?' he checked, and he took her hand to move it to the sheet beneath which he was hardening, but she resisted and her palm came to rest on his flat stomach.

There was no solace there for his skin was warm and she could feel the silk hair that led from his navel to paradise and she ached to move her hand lower.

So much had changed since yesterday.

Not just that she was leaving.

And not just that they had slept together.

He was creeping further into her heart.

'Luka, I really think we should just draw a neat line under what happened and when you come back from Xanero we'll go back to how we were.'

She was trying so hard to hold onto her heart, while at the same time sitting on his bed and looking into his eyes.

He pulled her head towards him, and she let him, and they shared a lingering kiss. He was leaving this morning, Cecelia told herself.

Order would soon be returned.

Just not yet.

Their tongues explored each other and their mouths were hungry for sensations.

He kissed down her neck and then moved the collar of her linen jacket and kissed the shoulders that had been revealed to him only yesterday, tracing her clavicle with his tongue until her neck arched.

'Don't leave a bruise...' she said, but he ignored her, biting into her flesh and sucking as his hand pushed between her thighs, which were pressed together.

'Come to bed,' Luka said.

And without hesitation she nodded.

Cecelia stood and his eyes were on her as she undressed. He watched as the navy jacket came off and he just stared as she removed her top to reveal the purple mark on her shoulder.

She slipped off her skirt and sandals and then straightened up and removed her bra. She could see he was hard beneath the sheet, and, in response to the command from her hungry eyes, he kicked it off.

He loved that he did not have to persuade her—that he did not have to slowly remove her bra and kiss her while sliding down her knickers.

Instead, she took care of that.

For this was no accident.

Her delicately shaped curls, which he had not had time to appreciate last night, had a coppery tinge that he stared at as she removed her bra. For the first time in years he was hungry to taste a woman, and reached for her to join him in bed.

'After this morning…' she warned, but he hushed her with his mouth. 'I mean it, Luka,' Cecelia said, pulling hers away.

'Sure,' he agreed, 'so this morning we make the most of it.'

Instead of kissing her, he knelt and lowered his head to her breast.

His tongue swirled around her nipple while his mouth closed and created a delicious vacuum. He sucked hard and Cecelia felt herself clench down below.

'Luka…'

'Nice?' he asked, removing his mouth and blowing on her erect nipple. Cecelia didn't know how to answer.

It was beyond nice, it was bliss, yet his moves were so practised and sure. She closed her eyes and then his mouth moved down her stomach.

'Am I getting the full Luka Kargas treatment?' she asked.

There was a moment of arrested silence while he paused, his mouth hovering over her stomach. What she didn't know was that in Luka's world the tables had turned many years ago. He no longer went down on women.

His start had been sex and Luka had long ago perfected his routine.

But now that his wealth exceeded theirs…

Well, he paid for *their* favours.

Not directly, of course.

With jewels and exotic weekends.

Now *they* went down on *him* instead of the other way around.

But not this morning.

It had been years since…

Years since *her* pleasure had mattered.

This morning it did.

'No,' he responded to her question. 'You're getting me.'

He kissed her stomach, not lightly but as deeply and intently as if it were her mouth, and Cecelia found her breath held in her throat as his hand slid between her closed legs. 'Open them.'

She did, just a little, and she lay there, determined almost not to enjoy it. To remind herself that this was his skill.

His thumb was intent and his fingers were inside her but Cecelia's throat was tight as he teased and stroked and rubbed, for she brought up her knees in an involuntary movement.

Women had paid him for this, she told herself as his tongue set to work alongside his thumb.

There was a moan building but she held onto it, yet he read it, for he moved between her legs to increase the intensity.

Luka heard her low moan and forgot his practised moves of old for this was new.

He heard her gasps, and finally learned the scent and taste of Cecelia on his tongue.

Her thighs were shaking as he probed deeply, and her hand pressed on his head, pushing him away. He knew she resisted pleasure.

So he upped the intensity again.

'Luka...' she sobbed, because it was too intense. His tongue was penetrating and he growled—and knew the moment she felt it. She wanted to come, but knew she would come so deeply that she was terrified to let herself go.

'Come, Cece,' he said, his voice rumbling through her. It was a command, an order her body could not ignore. Her back arched and her orgasm shot through her like lightning and earthed to his mouth.

He coaxed every flicker from her so that she was flushed and near crying when her body came down.

Never had it tasted this good. This was not like the work he used to do. This was different.

He slid up her body, Cecelia pulling him those final inches. They drank from each other in a desperate kiss that was both deep and heady. Luka came up on his arms but she pulled his head back down to claim a deeper kiss.

It was nothing like either of them had known before.

He was practised to the core and she was so new to passion, yet it was fire that they made together. She did not want him to be this good.

'That *wasn't* work,' he told her. 'That was bliss.'

And so was this.

He was there at her entrance and nudging a little way in. 'Come with me,' he said to the shell of her ear. 'To Xanero...'

Luka did not want to go and now had been presented with a way to make it more bearable.

She liked the thought of fourteen nights of this. But she held back.

'No,' she said, and he pulled out. 'I mean, no to Xanero...'

But yes to this.

Her eyes were closed as he slid in deep, all the way in. If she could have examined her thoughts she feared she would rediscover her self-control, and the part of her that knew this was wrong.

And so did Luka.

But they were past caring.

The feel of him unsheathed and stretching her was sublime.

And for Luka too, for she was slippery yet tight. He drove in deep and she let out a moan that he wanted to turn into a scream.

He reached for her leg and wrapped her calf around his thigh, pushing into her again. She was more open than she had ever been.

He thrust slowly and could feel the intimate welcoming grip of her.

Her nails dug into his buttocks and she moved with him until they were lost to each other and the moment.

'Luka…' She could barely breathe, yet at her plea he took her harder and faster, making her dizzy. She could feel her climax building and this time she welcomed it.

He angled himself and took her deeper and then he tipped into rapid, rhythmic thrusts from which there was no return. It was her scream that brought him back to consciousness.

It was her first scream in bed, Luka knew as his stomach lifted and he pulsed into her, shouting his release.

Her cry came from a place she had never known, and her orgasm was so intense that for a moment she felt possessed. As if her body had been taken over by someone else, by a woman who knew how to be free.

Yet as she gloried in the sensation, his weight atop her reminded her starkly that soon she would have to dig her way out of the ashes from the fire he had brought to her heart.

CHAPTER SIX

'COME WITH ME to Xanero.'

As the mist was clearing he said it again. His weight pressed down on her even as he still rested inside her. If there was ever a weak moment this was it and Cecelia knew she was about to say yes when Luka spoke.

'Not to the resort or anything,' he added, pushing up onto his forearms. 'Or my mother would think we were serious or something. You could stay on the yacht.'

Cecelia slid out from under him and rolled to her side. He did the same.

She had almost said yes.

In a delicious weak moment she had almost succumbed, and she failed to keep the bitter edge from her tone when she responded to his invitation. 'You mean, come to Xanero as your plaything.'

'I'd work you by day...' He smiled, completely unfazed as he toyed with her breast, still throbbing from his previous attention, for this was the life he led. 'And then make up for it by night.'

'So while you're on the island I'd be cooped up—'

'Hardly cooped up. It's not a tin boat with a gas stove....'

'I have seen your yacht, Luka.'

Well, she had seen pictures of it and had seen some

of the accounts for it. It was a luxury resort in itself, and of course she knew all about the wild parties that were held there.

And now she was being invited into the playboy's bed.

Oh, the dewy mist of his lovemaking was most certainly starting to clear for suddenly Cecelia pulled herself away and sat up.

And it was then that realisation kicked in. 'Luka, we didn't use anything…'

In a life spent not making mistakes, Cecelia had just made a huge one and there was no excuse.

For either of them.

'Are you on the Pill?'

'Yes, I'm on the Pill,' she snapped as she tried to remember if she'd taken it last night, because it hadn't just been putting out her clothes for the morning that had fallen by the wayside. But surely if she went home now and took it, then she'd be fine.

But pregnancy wasn't the only thing on her mind.

'It's not just that, though.' Cecelia turned and looked over to where he lay and saw that his expression was equally grim.

He'd just told her he'd once been a gigolo—she could not believe she had been so careless.

'Cecelia, you don't have to worry about anything there,' Luka said as he moved to reassure her. 'I *always* use protection.'

'Well, clearly you don't!'

It was as much her fault as his, Cecelia knew that, and her angry tone was aimed more towards herself.

'You'll be fine,' he said, which might have sounded dismissive, but neither did he want to admit just how impossibly rare this lapse was.

She gave a terse nod and headed for the shower while Luka lay there, his hands behind his head, trying to fathom what had just taken place.

This morning he'd forgotten the rules. This morning he'd been so wrapped in the feel of her, the feel of *them*, that he'd forgotten the care he usually took.

He had complete control in the bedroom, for though he was wild he was not reckless.

Yet this morning he had been.

Not only had he invited her to come to Xanero with him—at least he had quickly reacted and told Cece that she would only be on the yacht—but for a moment he had glimpsed it. His dream, showing off the first Kargas restaurant and the now stunning resort which was by far his proudest achievement to date.

And he had told her how his ascent to the top had started.

Luka wasn't particularly close to anyone.

He kept work and family neatly separated, and certainly he had never invited an employee, albeit one who had resigned, to join him there.

The yacht was for escape, for parties and fun. It had never been used as a couples' retreat.

She came out of the shower and dressed quickly. He was relieved that she seemed as keen to leave as he now wanted her gone, for she had messed with his head.

'I'd better take your case in to the office,' Cecelia said.

'Please.' He nodded. 'I'll be in later.'

No, he wasn't a perfect gentleman, for he did not tell her to leave the case and that he would take it.

And neither would his driver magically appear.

She could take the underground.

Cecelia had said herself that she wanted to draw a neat line and get back to being his PA.

That suited him just fine.

Last night had been amazing.

So had this morning, and yet now he was left feeling deeply unsettled.

Luka chose not to get close to anyone, but this morning he had.

Xanero really was hell in paradise.

For Luka, the first week there had been a protracted nightmare—his mother seemed resigned to her fate and his father continued to lord it over the restaurant and resort.

And he had found out that his father was bullying the staff.

Bastard!

While Luka disliked how his father had rewritten history to suit the image of himself he wanted to believe, Luka could live with it if it made life easier on his mother.

But bullying would not happen in one of Luka's establishments, and for all the lies and wealth that shaped his mother's life, she was finding it no easier that he could see.

Luka had taken the yacht out over the weekend, but the pop of champagne corks and the sound of music skimming over the Mediterranean had soon grated and he had cleared everyone off except the crew as he mulled things over. Now, back on Xanero, and midway through the second week, on the Wednesday morning his decisions were made and he was ready to execute them.

He walked through the alfresco area of the restaurant where diners were enjoying the morning sun and through to the cool darkness of the main restaurant.

Theo Kargas was at the bar, speaking with the bar manager, and Luka could feel the young man's tension from across the room.

'Hey,' he said to his father. 'We need to talk.'

'About?' Theo asked, even as he crammed whitebait, crisped to perfection, into his mouth. He was utterly relaxed, for any angry words from his son always took place out of earshot of the staff.

Yes, Luka's door was always closed.

Not so today.

'I want to discuss your appalling treatment of my staff and your inexcusable conduct towards my mother.'

Theo almost choked, but then attempted a recovery. '*Your* staff? We are partners. I gave you—'

'You gave me nothing,' Luka said, and got right in his father's face. 'You actually believe your own lies. Now, as I said, we need to talk…' He gestured to a table, for he too would prefer privacy for this but the fact he had first addressed the issues in front of the bar manager had been deliberate.

Theo *would* listen, or Luka *would* act.

'I bought this restaurant,' Luka said, 'from the money I made picking up rich woman…'

'Luka,' his father warned, for a waiter was setting up the table and could hear what was being said.

'What?' Luka shrugged. 'I'm not ashamed of it.'

Well, perhaps he was a bit, but having told Cecelia the real truth about his start he felt more reconciled with it.

So he told his father a truth that had consistently been ignored. 'I gave you an opportunity to work, and you spurned it. I have put up with it for years for my mother's sake. No more. I am hiring a new manager, who shall report directly to me. One more episode of your foul temper used on my staff and I shall take you through the courts to extricate you from our agreement and the restaurant's name shall be changed to Luka Kargas.'

'It would kill your mother.'

'She's already dying,' Luka pointed out, and then he looked right at his father. 'Actually, she isn't, because I am moving her to London for her treatments and I am going to ensure that she rests and is taken care of between them.'

'You can't just swan in here and dictate—'

'Oh, but I can,' Luka said. 'I own the complex, and I have a half-share in the restaurant, and,' he added, 'I can destroy you if I so choose. You should be pleading with your wife to seek treatment, because if it wasn't for her you'd be seeing your days out in a shack on the hills and, believe me, Theo, you don't want to test me on that.'

'I'm your father!' Theo reared and stood and leant across the table and grabbed Luka's shirt.

'More's the pity,' Luka said. 'And I strongly suggest that you get your hands off me. I'm not ten years old any more, or a skinny teenager up against a brute. I could floor you and I am more than willing to do it.'

Sensibly, his father removed his hand, for it was clear Luka meant every word. But he was not finished yet. 'You have no idea the ruthless bastard I can be. I could crush you and your so-called empire in the palm of my hand,' Luka said. 'And I will say it again, just so we're clear—the *only* reason I've held back where the resort is concerned is for the sake of my mother.'

It was Luka who stood up and walked off back towards his villa.

He'd have loved to have hit his bully of a father,

but what good could come from that? So instead he stripped off and dived into the pool, pounding out several lengths before hauling himself from the water a touch breathless.

And then he messaged Cecelia.

We need to talk.

His message came up on her computer and Cecelia tensed, because though they had spoken about work both online and on the phone on many occasions, this sounded rather personal.

She replied quickly.

I'm about to call someone in for an interview.

So?

Of course he didn't mean that they needed to speak about what had taken place between them, Cecelia scolded herself for her less-than-professional reply. If Luka Kargas wanted to speak to his PA it didn't matter if she'd been about to call someone in.

'I have to speak with Mr Kargas,' Cecelia said to the interviewee. 'I'll be back when I can.'

Cecelia didn't apologise for keeping Sabine waiting, for the potential PA might as well get a glimpse of what she would be in for.

A moment later his face appeared on her screen and Cecelia got more than a glimpse.

His chest was naked and her view was of a dark mahogany nipple surrounded by a swirl of black hair. But then he angled the screen better and she saw that his hair was wet and he was squinting from the bright sun.

'What can I do for you?' Cecelia asked.

Her voice was cool, her demeanour brisk and she was determined that they were back to business.

'What are you doing?' he asked.

'Working.' She frowned. 'Marco has a few things he needs to run by you but apart from that things are ticking along.'

She was wearing a grey dress with a sheer grey silky cardigan, because perish the thought that she might show too much skin. Her hair was neat and pulled back and yet now he knew another side to her he couldn't help but see her buttoned-up appearance for what it was. A defence strategy.

'I want you to fly here,' Luka said. 'I want you here tonight.'

Cecelia stared back at him. 'For work?'

'No.'

She liked it that he was direct.

In fact, Cecelia liked it that he had basically asked her to get on a plane for sex. But what happened when he got bored? She reminded herself of all the reasons she had refused his original offer.

He would wake up one morning and instead of kisses she would sense his restlessness.

His slight disdain.

Oh, she had seen it on too many occasions not to know what was in store for her.

At least here in London she was but a taxi ride away from salvaging her pride when he told her they were through.

But in Xanero?

Did she book her own flight home?

Or would they suffer it through until she left his employ less than three weeks from now?

'If it isn't for work, then I shan't be joining you.'

'Fine,' Luka snapped. 'In that case, I need you to go and view some apartments for me.'

'Sure.'

'And I want you to interview some private nurses. Make sure they speak Greek.'

Cecelia took down the details.

It was now all very businesslike. Surly, but businesslike. Yet she ached to know more about his mother, though she resisted asking for details that were not with the remit of a professional relationship.

They had spent one night together, and she knew from his reputation that that didn't give her the keys to his private life.

'How are the interviews for your replacement going?' Luka asked.

'I'm getting there,' Cecelia said. 'I'm on the second round, so I should have a shortlist of three for you to choose from.'

'Any stand-outs?'

Cecelia hesitated.

Luka was a demanding boss but she almost had to shake the stars from potential employees' eyes to ensure they understood what the job entailed.

But one had stood out.

Sabine.

She had an incredible work history and was bright and engaging. The only trouble was that Cecelia didn't like her.

'There's one,' Cecelia said. 'Sabine. I'm just about to interview her again and give her a tour but...'

'But what?'

'I don't know,' Cecelia admitted.

'Try telling me.'

'I don't like her.' Cecelia shrugged. 'But, then, she's not for me to like. I'll see how this interview goes. She speaks Greek, which might be a help with your mother, and...'

'My mother will be coming to London for treatment, not for little get-togethers with my PA.'

He turned off the computer and closed it up.

Luka really did not want her to leave.

And yet it was perhaps for the best because despite strong words about PAs not getting involved with his family, he had told Cecelia some things he had never told anyone. And he had her interviewing nurses and looking for apartments.

He trusted her, and Luka was more comfortable trusting no one.

With that awkward conversation over, Cecelia got on with the second-round interviews.

Cecelia was self-aware enough to know that it was probably for private reasons that she couldn't take to Sabine. The young woman was gorgeous, with piercing blue eyes and straight black hair cut in a jagged, edgy style. She made Cecelia feel terribly drab.

'Luka will probably call you Sab, or Sabby...' Cecelia said in an offhand comment as she showed her around. 'It drives me crazy.'

'He can call me what he likes as long as he pays me.'

Cecelia held in a breath.

Sabine was arrogant and overly confident perhaps, but she really was the perfect match for Luka.

She could almost hear the banter between them.

'This is his suite,' Cecelia explained as she opened the door. 'It's serviced daily but I tend to check it as it sometimes needs an extra service. Not currently, though, he's still in Greece.'

'So I read!' Sabine said.

Cecelia had been doing her level best not to read about him, but once the interviews were wrapped up she found that she could not resist.

The headlines were all in the same vein: *Xanero Magnate Returns.*

It would seem that the weekend had been spent out on his yacht and she knew full well what went on on board.

She clicked on the article and there were the glossy beauties that always surrounded him and the sun hanging low in a fiery sky.

Luka didn't even wait for nightfall to get a party started.

It wasn't just the resumption of his sex life that concerned her, though—oh, but it did, *desperately* it did—but also what had happened that morning between them.

Cecelia could not believe she'd had unprotected sex. Though she kept willing herself calm, yesterday she had caved and made an appointment with her GP.

At the conclusion of the interview today Cecelia was heading there.

'Well, thank you for coming in,' Cecelia said as she walked Sabine to the elevator. 'You can expect to hear from me by the end of the week.'

'I'll look forward to it.' Sabine smiled and the women shook hands.

Cecelia really didn't like her, but it would seem she was the only one to feel so.

'She seems really nice,' Bridgette commented as Cecelia walked back from the elevator.

Yes, it was probably for rather personal reasons that

she didn't like her, Cecelia guessed, and decided that she would be putting Sabine forward.

Luka could make the final call.

'I'm going out for a couple of hours,' she told Bridgette. 'I won't have my phone on.'

'What should I say if Luka calls because he can't get hold of you?' Bridgette checked, because his PA was always supposed to be available.

'Tell him I'm…' She didn't know what to say. 'Tell him I'm taking a long lunch.'

Lunch didn't come into it.

Instead, she took the underground until she was practically home and spent the next hour sitting in the waiting room at her GP's surgery.

Cecelia was rarely there and finally, when her name was called, she rather hoped she would be in and out in a few minutes with her mind eased.

Dr Heale introduced herself and Cecelia told her the reason she was there.

'It's probably nothing,' Cecelia started. 'In fact, I'm sure I'm wasting your time…'

'Why don't you let me be the judge of that?'

Very well.

Why was discussing sex always so awkward for her? The shame came from her aunt and uncle, Cecelia knew. They spoke in whispers and were still mortified by the salacious circumstances in which her mother had died.

Cecelia did her best to push all that aside and to speak in a matter-of-fact tone. 'I had unprotected sex last week.'

'When?'

'On Monday night,' Cecelia said. 'Or rather on the Tuesday morning.'

'You're on the Pill?' Dr Heale checked, reading through her notes.

'Yes,' Cecelia said, 'though I usually take my Pill at night…'

'And you didn't?'

'No.'

'Well, you've left it too late for the morning-after pill.'

She hadn't really thought about it the morning after, but now Dr Heale was telling her that she'd had a window of a week.

That window was closed to her now.

'But it's probably fine?' Cecelia pushed, only Dr Heale wasn't exactly rushing to put her at ease; in fact, she was reading Cecelia's notes.

'Are you still with your fiancé?' she asked.

Cecelia remembered the last time she had been there, carefully going on the Pill before she and Gordon did anything.

There had certainly been no up-against-the-wall sex with him!

'Er, no.'

'Do you have a new partner?'

'Not exactly,' Cecelia croaked. 'It was a one-off, well…'

'That's fine,' Dr Heale said. 'But with a casual encounter it is, of course, more important that you're careful.'

She was right, except there was nothing casual about Cecelia's feelings for Luka.

And there was that sting of shame again—not that Dr Heale turned a hair. If anything, she was very practical.

'Perhaps, while you're here, we should run a sexual health check,' she suggested.

It looked like Cecelia would not be in and out in a

couple of minutes; in fact, she returned from lunch a full hour late.

'Luka's been calling the office,' Bridgette warned. 'And he's not best pleased that your mobile's turned off.'

He certainly had been calling, Cecelia thought when she turned it back on. She had barely sat down before he called again.

'How was the dentist?' he asked, and there was an edge to Luka's voice for he was quite sure where she had been.

'Excuse me?' Cecelia flared.

'You're the one making up excuses. Were you off visiting your new office? Or perhaps having lunch with your new boss—whoever that may be?'

'No,' Cecelia calmly responded. 'I had an appointment. Now, what can I do for you?'

You can get here, Luka wanted to answer.

He had never had to chase or pursue, and the one woman who could have made him feel better had distanced herself from him.

'How did the second-round interviews go?'

'Very well. I have a shortlist of three for you to interview.'

'Bring them in early next week.'

'So you'll be back on Monday?' Cecelia checked.

But Luka had already rung off.

CHAPTER SEVEN

CECELIA KNEW HE was back the very second she stepped out of the elevator.

That tangy citrus scent of him had never really left the place but it was stronger today.

There was a knot of tight nerves in her stomach and she had no idea how to play this. She sensed he had come out of his office as she hung up her jacket, and this was confirmed when she heard him speak.

'Hi.'

His voice was low and deep and, though expected, she still had to fight not to jump. Instead she turned around at his greeting.

He looked amazing, and even if he had gone home to deal with a difficult situation it was clear there had been time spent in the sun.

'Hi, Luka.'

'How are things?'

'Great. But Mr Garcia is insisting that you speak with him today.'

'Tell him I can fit him in tomorrow.'

'Very well,' Cecelia said as she held in a sigh. 'And you have the applicants for my replacement coming in between two and four.'

'Good.'

He'd hoped she might reconsider, given what had taken place, but deep down he knew she wouldn't have.

Cecelia was professional, and even Luka, who in the past had happily slept with his PA, knew that a line had been crossed and that it would be impossible to go back to the way they had been.

For once he did not want to talk about work.

Neither did he want to hit the computer.

After a hellish two weeks at home, quite simply he wanted to take her to bed.

Instead, there was a lot to do.

The head of his legal team was in and out of his office all morning, and Marco, head of accounting, was there too. From what she could glean, Luka was looking to sever business ties with his father.

As his mother battled cancer!

Luka's ruthlessness made her shiver.

It was approaching one o'clock when Cecelia told him that an apartment she had seen would be available for him to view this evening.

'I shan't be going ahead with that.'

'Oh.'

He had asked his mother to come to London and concentrate on surviving but the answer had been no.

She had at least agreed to have treatments in Athens, on the condition she could return home after each course.

Luka rather guessed they were his father's conditions but his efforts to persuade her otherwise had fallen on deaf ears.

At least she wasn't simply giving up now, but Luka knew that he had to do more.

He had spent the morning testing the legal waters

with his team, but it would be long and protracted to have his father forcibly removed as joint owner.

And he did not want the extra stress on his mother.

In fact, Luka, who dreaded going home, even for the occasional weekend, was starting to realise that Xanero might soon have to act as his base, at least for a while.

'You said one of the applicants spoke Greek?' Luka checked.

'Yes, Sabine.'

'And she is okay with extensive travel?'

'Yes.' Cecelia nodded. 'But, Luka, I really think Kelly, the first applicant, is more suitable.'

'Does she speak Greek?'

'No,' Cecelia said, 'but then neither do I.'

'There's a lot of things you don't do,' Luka said, and from the curl of his mouth and the charge in the air, the meaning was explicitly clear.

'Don't!' Cecelia warned. She had been wondering how they would play this and if the past would be politely ignored—well, clearly not.

And Cecelia was furious.

'I'm the best bloody PA you have ever had and don't you dare forget it. Just because I won't hop on a plane to Xanero for a shag...' Her face was on fire as he stared right back and gave her a black smile, so she upped it. 'Or get down on my knees and blow you under the desk...' She knew he was hard and she was wet too, but, hell, he had brought it to work, and she wasn't going to back down now. 'It doesn't mean I'm not brilliant at my work. Don't forget that, Luka.'

He was saved from a smart answer when her phone rang and Cecelia glanced at it to see who was calling.

'Go ahead,' Luka said, but Cecelia shook her head.

'It's fine.'

She would not be taking a call from her doctor in front of Luka, especially given the nature of the tests last week! Instead she excused herself, returned to the privacy of her desk and called the surgery.

'This is Cecelia Andrews,' she said to the receptionist. 'A message was left, asking me to call.'

'One moment, please.'

It was closer to two moments and they were possibly the longest of her life.

'The doctor would like to see you to go over your test results.'

'I'm actually at work and it's terribly hard to get away. If I could speak with the doctor…'

'We have a policy that we don't give results over the phone. I have a vacancy next Monday at two fifteen.'

'Monday!' Cecelia yelped. There was no way she could wait.

'Actually, there's just been a cancellation for today at one thirty. If you can get here by then, it's yours.'

'I shall,' Cecelia said, and did her best to remember her manners as the world imploded on her. 'And thank you.'

Luka came out then with work on his mind. 'If you could call the Athens team now…'

'It's my lunch break,' Cecelia cut in, and Luka blinked.

'Well, get something sent up and eat at your desk. I need this sorted.'

'Luka,' she said, 'I'm entitled to a lunch break, and I'm taking it.'

She was panicking now, remembering his salacious past and what that could mean for her.

She headed to the bathroom and when she returned

he saw that she had redone her hair and refreshed her make-up.

'Good luck,' he said as she walked out.

'Excuse me?' She turned around, wondering if he had guessed where she was going.

'With your new boss.' His voice was tart. 'I assume that's where you're headed.'

Cecelia said nothing.

'Just make sure you're back on time. I believe you're *entitled* to an hour.'

She hated this.

Cecelia absolutely hated this. She should never have got involved with her boss and now everything had changed.

Bristling, Cecelia took the elevator down and with no time to lose she raced for the underground and made it just in time for her appointment, where they asked her to give another urine sample.

And then she sat for the longest half-hour of her life, thumbing blindly through magazines.

Until suddenly her eye was caught by a shot of Luka, pelvis to pelvis with some beauty and dancing the night away in Barcelona. Admittedly, it was an old magazine, though it was not the type of thing she needed to see right now.

'Cecelia Andrews?'

She put down the magazine and stood up, deciding she would kill him with her bare hands if he'd given her anything.

It was the same doctor she had seen the previous week and Cecelia sat as Dr Heale went through her notes.

'I've had a look through your results and I thought it better that I see you face to face.'

Cecelia felt her heart plummet.

'All the health checks came back clear. However, I asked you to repeat the urine specimen as your BHCG came back as elevated.'

'What does that mean?' Cecelia asked, her mind swinging from one horror to another.

'It's very early days,' the doctor said, 'but the second test confirms that you are pregnant.'

'The other tests…?' Cecelia asked for she could not take it in.

'They're all clear.'

'But I'm on the Pill—' Cecelia started, but then the high horse she had been sitting on while blaming Luka for any misfortune that might come to bear on her shifted.

This predicament really was down to her.

She had missed a pill, and at the very least should have looked into the morning-after pill while there was still time for it to be effective.

A baby was the very last thing Cecelia wanted.

She would be a single mother.

Just like her mum.

And she would be single, that much she could guarantee.

'I'm only just, though…' Cecelia vainly attempted, unsure what she was even saying. 'Two weeks.'

'Four weeks,' the doctor clarified. 'Your levels are spot on. It's calculated from the first day of your last period.'

Cecelia screwed her eyes closed. A little over two weeks ago they hadn't even kissed.

Yet now she was being told that she was four weeks pregnant.

By Luka Kargas who was, by any account, the biggest rake known.

'I don't know what to do,' Cecelia admitted. 'I honestly don't know how I feel.'

'Of course you don't,' Dr Heale said. 'Why don't you make an appointment with me for next week and by then the news will have had time to sink in a bit.'

Cecelia did just that and then she made her way out of the clinic. She stood on the busy London street full of people who were carrying on with their day, oblivious to the bombshell that had dropped on her world.

She wiped her cheeks with her hand and only then did Cecelia realise she was crying.

It was as if all her emotions were in full flight, for there were tears and her heart was hammering in her chest, yet Cecelia was barely aware of them.

'Numb.'

She said it out loud just to hear her own voice and to clarify that it was how she felt.

Numb.

She could hear her phone ringing but it did not even enter her head to answer it. Instead she walked and walked through London streets, carrying her bag in her hand rather than in its usual position over her shoulder.

A baby?

It had not been in her plans—at least, not her current plans.

Even when she and Gordon had spoken about one day having children it had been a sort of dim and distant thing in the far-away future, and even then she hadn't really been able to picture it.

Her career was the most important thing in her life. It was the only thing she really had, but how the hell was she going to be able to carry on with it with a baby?

Luka would carry on.

A baby wouldn't affect *his* career.

The numbness was fading and the sting of sensation was coming back as she briefly envisaged Luka's reaction if she told him the news.

And the aftermath.

She had worked with him for almost a year and knew the bastard he could be. As recently as this morning he'd had his legal and accounting teams working out how to screw over his own father.

She could not stand to think of the meeting that would take place about her if he found out about the baby!

Cecelia walked into a bar and ordered a glass of water. She sat on a stool but the world would not stop spinning.

She started a new job in a couple of weeks' time.

It was only a six-month contract, though.

Which would take her up to seven months pregnant.

Really, she could not have planned it better, except she had not planned on being pregnant at all.

Her phone was ringing again and, unthinking, she answered it.

'Where the hell are you?' Luka demanded. 'Bridgette's gone home with a migraine and I'm playing receptionist to my potential PAs!'

'You'll have to manage without me,' Cecelia said, for there was no way she could go back to work this afternoon and face him. Even keeping her voice remotely normal was taking a supreme effort.

He heard the chink of glasses and a burst of laughter in the background and the effort behind her words. He could picture her with her new boss, all cosy on some sofa in a club. 'You still have two weeks left to serve your notice, Cecelia. I suggest that you get back here now.'

'And I just told you that I can't.'

She was not being defiant, there was just absolutely no way she could make it into work.

He rang off and Cecelia sat watching a woman wheeling in her baby in a pram, wrestling with the glass doors.

It was not her world.

Meanwhile, Luka sat and stared at his phone.

It was not a world he was used to either and, as Luka quickly found out, rejection was certainly not his forte.

He did not kill her with kindness.

Cecelia arrived at work the following morning and nodded to the doorman.

She made her way up in the elevator and again saw that she had beaten Bridgette to it.

Yet she was not the first here.

Or the second.

Her desk had been moved. And it was not arranged the way she usually left it.

There was a laptop on it that wasn't hers and when she went behind it there was a bag on the floor that felt like finding the wrong shoes by the bed.

She had spent the night fighting not just whether or not to tell him but, if she did, how.

He had, she realised, removed the opportunity to do so.

'Cecelia.'

She turned to the low, familiar sound of his voice and the clipped tones at Luka's unfamiliar correct usage of her name.

'I have hired your replacement.'

'So I see.'

'There is no need for you to stay on.'

'What about…?' Her mind darted to the million and one things she needed to pass on. 'There's the Athens—'

'Sorted,' Luka interrupted. 'Of course, you shall be paid while *not* serving your notice.'

'And this is because I didn't return from lunch?'

'No, this is because of your attitude.'

'Am I back at school?' Cecelia flared.

'Did you have an attitude problem then?' Luka smoothly responded.

No, she hadn't had an attitude problem at school.

She'd been diligent and hard-working and had toed the line, determined that her life would be different from her mother's.

And neither had she had an attitude at home, for she'd been trying so hard not to get in her aunt and uncle's way.

Her attitude only changed when she was with him.

Luka brought out both the best and the worst in her.

And he was the worst.

She knew that, and it was proved when Sabine came out.

She had the grace to offer a somewhat awkward smile in Cecelia's direction.

Her black hair was a little messy, like she had a case of bedhead… It appeared they had worked through the night.

Or otherwise.

Cecelia didn't trust Luka enough not to consider *otherwise*.

And Cecelia knew then the answer to the problem she had wrestled with since the doctor had delivered the baby bombshell to her.

No way would she tell him.

She did not want her child subjected to the life he led.

Cecelia knew from experience the damage that could cause.

And if he could snuff her out of his life overnight, if he could so calmly watch as Sabine handed her a package with all her things and escorted her out, then he could easily do the same to his child.

CHAPTER EIGHT

THE DECISION ABOUT whether to tell him was not, of course, as clear cut as that.

For the first couple of months a generous dash of anger fired Cecelia's spirit, for she certainly hadn't deserved that.

How dared he have Sabine walk her out of the office? How dared he question her attitude, when he was the most arrogant person on earth?

Her anger, combined with a healthy dose of denial as to the truth of her predicament, got Cecelia through the first trimester of her pregnancy.

Cecelia did consider a termination, but in the end could not see herself going through with it.

Her father had wanted her mother to abort her, and she was also rather certain that Luka would suggest the same.

So she hid the news from the world and worked hard in her new job.

As long as she didn't show, she could work hard and pretend that nothing had changed.

At first she enjoyed the life where sixteen or more hours of her day were not devoted to Luka's exhausting schedule, and eight hours of night time were not spent rejecting the hunger of her body for him.

Except she lied, for now she had experienced him, it was not fantasy that peppered her thoughts and dreams but intoxicating memories.

Unlike Luka, her new diplomat boss was so stunningly politically correct that he made no mention of her expanding waistline. But as Christmas approached, Cecelia formally told him that she would not be renewing her contract at the end of her term.

Cecelia had always been sensible with money and had some savings, but she was starting to glimpse how impossible it would be to combine her regular work with motherhood.

Anxiety about the future woke Cecelia up in the middle of the night, and of course there were times that she considered telling Luka.

But not like this, Cecelia thought as she nervously headed to her aunt and uncle's house to tell them the news. Not when her heart was fluttering in fear and she was constantly on the edge of tears.

On the Tube she checked her hair and make-up and could see the anxiety in her own eyes in the mirror as she tried to fathom how they would take it.

'Cecelia.' Her aunt frowned when she opened the front door to her niece. 'You didn't call to say you were dropping by.'

Should she have to? Cecelia thought, but as usual said nothing.

And neither did she remove her coat.

She sat in the drawing room as tea was served and felt as uncomfortable as she had on the day she had first arrived here.

It was a very austere house and Cecelia could remember sitting on this very seat as her grandfather had spoken with his son about boarding school for her.

'How's work?' her aunt asked.

'It's going well.' Cecelia nodded. 'The hours are much better than in my previous job. However, I've told him that I shan't be renewing my contract.'

'Have you found something else?' her aunt asked.

Cecelia took a sip of tea and then replaced the cup in the saucer and made herself say it. 'No, I shan't be working for a few months because I've found out that I'm expecting.' When her aunt said nothing, Cecelia made things a touch clearer. 'A baby.'

'I wasn't aware you'd been dating since the break-up.'

'Gordon and I finished more than a year ago,' Cecelia attempted, but she felt her face flush, because what had happened that night with Luka couldn't even be described as a date, let alone a relationship.

They weren't a couple.

Quite simply, it had been the most impulsive night of her life.

And as for the morning…

Cecelia forced herself not to dwell on that. Right now she had to get through telling her aunt.

'My contract expires a couple of months before the baby is due and I can afford to take a few months off.'

'So what does the father have to say on the matter?'

'I haven't told him,' Cecelia admitted. 'Yet.'

Deep down Cecelia knew she had to tell Luka, but for now she was trying to get used to the idea herself. Certainly she did not want to be teary and hysterical when she told him the news, which was frankly how she felt most of the time.

Not that Cecelia showed it. As always, she appeared outwardly calm.

Yes, it might be a difficult conversation to have with her aunt but Cecelia hoped that she would soon come round.

And then hope died.

She watched as her aunt added another spoon of sugar to her tea and stirred, and then placed the spoon on the saucer.

The silence had been a long one and Cecelia did not attempt to fill it. Instead, she stayed quiet to allow her aunt to process the news. When she did, her eyes met Cecelia's.

'The apple doesn't fall far from the tree, does it? Well, I raised your mother's mistake,' she said. 'You need to know Cecelia that I shan't be doing it again for you.'

Cecelia felt a shiver run the length of her spine as she met her aunt's eyes, and in that moment the past twenty years or so made a little more sense.

She had never felt welcome here and now she knew why.

A mistake.

That was what her aunt had just called her.

Deep down, Cecelia had known it, for she had done all that she could not to make any trouble for her aunt and uncle and not to live up to her mother's reputation.

It would seem in her aunt's eyes she just had.

'I should go,' Cecelia said, polite to the very end. 'Please, give my love to my uncle.'

Instead of going home, Cecelia headed for her old workplace and sat in a café nearby, looking up at the towering high-rise that housed Kargas Holdings and wondering what to do.

A mistake.

Over and over it played in her mind.

They were the same words her father had used the one time she had seen him.

She tried to fathom Luka's reaction—she pictured his beautiful features marred by anger, and she imagined them locked in a bitter row, and right there in the café Cecelia started to cry.

She simply wasn't ready to reveal the pregnancy to him, Cecelia decided, if she was breaking down just imagining it.

No, she would tell Luka about the pregnancy when she felt calmer and when she could do it without being reduced to tears.

In the end, it was an uneventful but terribly lonely pregnancy.

Her six months working for the diplomat were soon up, and of course her contract was not renewed.

She was barely speaking to her aunt and uncle, and the few friends she had were somewhat aghast that she had gone ahead with the pregnancy.

Worse, though, she missed *him*.

Luka.

Not as the father of the baby she carried.

More, Cecelia missed the many different colours he had once added to her day.

She could feel the kicks of her baby, only it wasn't just duty that had her call Luka, it was the ache to hear his voice.

His private number must have been changed, for an automated voice told her to check the number and try again.

So she called the front desk and braced herself to speak with Bridgette or Sabine and to ask to be put through to Luka.

Instead it was an unfamiliar female voice she met with.

'I'm sorry, Mr Kargas isn't taking any unscheduled calls.'

'I used to work for him,' Cecelia explained. 'I was his PA and I—'

'As I said, Mr Kargas isn't taking any unscheduled calls.'

The voice was as brusque and efficient as Cecelia herself had once been when dealing with yet another slightly desperate female on the line.

'I have to speak with him,' Cecelia said. 'Can you let him know that I called?'

'Of course,' came the terse response. 'Can you spell your first name, please…'

He did not return the call.

It really was a terribly lonely time.

And now that Cecelia did not have work to occupy her, she caved under her broken heart for the first time.

She should have walked away at the outset.

Or she should never have turned to the huskiness of his voice that night.

Yet, even heavily pregnant, just the thought of the frantic sex that had taken place hit so low in her belly that she almost sank to her knees at the memory she could never erase.

But it hadn't even been that.

No, it was the morning after she would correct if she could.

She would peel away from his kiss and reach for a condom.

She would turn from his embrace and do things more sensibly.

Yet she could not see how, for she had been lost, *they* had been lost, and so deep into each other that even with the benefit of hindsight she could not play it another way, for she wanted him even now.

Spring came, and three weeks from her due date Cecelia tried to call him one more time.

'Mr Kargas isn't taking any unscheduled calls.'

'You sound like a broken record,' Cecelia snapped, and ended the call as she realised her pride had waned. Labour kind of did that to you, and perhaps mid-contraction wasn't the best time to tell him that she was having his child.

So she called for a taxi instead.

'Good luck, my dear,' Mrs Dawson called as Cecelia headed out.

'Thank you.'

Oh, it was lonely indeed.

And painful.

Cecelia wanted her old life back.

The ordered one.

The one she'd had prior to meeting Luka Kargas.

She did not want to be a mother, and certainly not a single one, so she sobbed through the pain and rued her mistakes.

But then, at ten minutes past six on a spring morning, for the second time in her life, Cecelia fell in love.

The first time had been with Luka.

There had never been anyone else in her life she had felt that way about, no one who came close.

But second-time love was the absolute shock of her life, for as she pulled the infant from her stomach into her arms, the world, in an instant, was put to right.

She had a daughter.

A tiny daughter who was very pink with a shock of dark hair and her cry was lusty and loud.

Oh!

Cecelia had told herself during the pregnancy that even if she felt little now, love would one day grow.

Her baby would never feel as unloved as her mother had been, even if she had to fake it for a while.

Yet there was never a love less fake, for Cecelia utterly adored her baby girl on sight.

'Have you thought of names?' the midwife asked as Cecelia gazed at her child.

'I liked Emily,' Cecelia said.

That had been before she had met her, though.

That was before she had locked eyes with a tiny, dark-haired, dark-eyed girl.

Her secret.

A secret she must one day reveal, Cecelia knew that.

But not yet.

She did not want the beauty of this tiny life marred just yet, she did not want the rows and accusations that would surely follow such a revelation.

The DNA tests, the lawyers, the disdain.

Cecelia could envisage it.

And that was at best.

She had nothing in her past to predict otherwise, and so she was in no rush to reveal to the billionaire playboy that she had birthed his child.

And she knew now her daughter's name.

It was, Cecelia knew, absolutely the perfect name for her and as she first said it she kissed her baby's soft cheek.

'Pandora.'

CHAPTER NINE

Summer had returned.

Luka had by far preferred the previous one.

But it was good to be home.

Yes, he thought of London as such.

Xanero was beautiful, and of course family was there, but it was London that was his true home.

Luka glanced up from the letter he was reading and looked out through tinted windows as his driver inched the car along the busy street.

He had been in London on occasion, but it been a hellish year on the private front, and the city had not been his base.

Amber, his ultra-efficient PA, had handed him a pile of personal correspondence and he wanted it dealt with before he turned his mind to work.

There was a pile of sympathy cards and letters that spoke of a hard-working family man that Luka did not recognise as his father.

'How was the funeral?' Amber asked.

'It went well,' Luka nodded.

Yesterday his father had been buried.

This time last year he had thought it would be his mother's funeral he would attend first, yet after months of intensive treatment and care, Sophie Kargas was doing well.

Luka had flown with her to Athens and after each treatment he would check them into the luxurious hotel he had there. Sophie had enjoyed the Princess Suite and had been treated exactly as that for the first time in her life.

'You could have this every day,' Luka had said. 'Say the word and I will take care of you and you will never have to deal with him.'

'I shall never do that, Luka,' his mother would reply.

Yet she was so much happier and lighter without him, and her decision to stay was something he would never quite understand.

And then, after each treatment, when her strength had returned they would go back to Xanero, where the new manager that Luka had hired would report directly to him.

Theo had reluctantly behaved, for he had been given no choice but to do so.

Luka had, quite literally, bought his mother a year of peace to focus on getting well.

There had been little peace for Luka, though— spending more time in Xanero had meant he'd been forced to face his demons.

No, he was not particularly proud of his start and he was tired too of the life he led.

And he regretted how he and Cece had parted.

Her decision to leave had been something he had not understood, in much the same way as his mother's decision to stay, and so he had hastened it. He had made sure she would not work out her notice and had her removed from his life in his usual style.

Yet he still thought about her each day.

And just when he had decided it was time to return to London, just when his life could get back on track and he was considering looking her up, completely out of the blue his father had died.

The funeral had been hell for Luka.

He had delivered the eulogy, and for his mother's sake he had spoken of the family man, his humble beginnings and the restaurant Theo had started. It had been a further rewriting of the past.

It was over with now.

'Is there anything—?' Amber started to ask.

But Luka cut in. 'Everything has been taken care of.'

His family life remained out of bounds to his PA.

Sabine had proved to be a nightmare.

He should have paid more attention when Cecelia had said there was something about her that she didn't like.

He had arrogantly assumed it was that Sabine was beautiful and had perhaps hoped that his hiring her would rouse a response in Cecelia.

Instead, his new PA had been the jealous one.

Sabine could not accept that he did not flirt and had no real interest in her, and when he had found her going through his private emails, he had fired her on the spot.

Amber had taken her place and, while she didn't speak Greek, he had no complaints. She was diligent and efficient and had no interest in sleeping her way to the top.

Yes, while there was nothing to complain about on the work front, he missed Cecelia.

In every way.

And never more so than this week.

He had arranged the funeral, dealt with the legalities and the only calls he had made to Amber had been regarding work.

His own mood even he could not begin to gauge.

There was a sense of relief tempered by unexpected grief.

He had no fond memories of his father, so it didn't really make sense, but there was a hollow feeling that resided within him now and an ache of sadness that he had not anticipated.

Yes, it had been a difficult year, though not on paper.

The talks with Garcia had become more productive and there was now a hotel and restaurant in Manhattan and another soon to open in Singapore. A lot of his time had been spent divided between Athens, where his mother had had her treatments, and Xanero, where she had recuperated in between.

The luxurious complex was large enough that he certainly had no need to temper his ways—after all, his family were hardly living over the fence.

He had tempered them, though.

Because he *still* wanted Cece.

Unable to face yet another sympathy card, he got back to staring out of the window.

And then Luka decided that it really had been too long, because he thought for a moment that a woman walking down the street might be her.

On too many occasions in the past year Luka had thought that he'd seen Cece.

Confidently he had once tapped a woman on the shoulder in a bar, and had then found himself staring into the wrong face.

But now, as he craned his neck for a better look, there was something about this woman's posture that held Luka's attention.

'Slow down,' he told his driver, because he no longer trusted himself to be certain when it came to her.

She looked slimmer, and the usually immaculate blonde hair that she wore tied back was more strawberry blonde and fell in untidy curls around her shoulders.

The uncertainty was short-lived, because he suddenly remembered the morning she had undressed for him and he had found out she was a redhead after all.

It really was her.

She wore a navy shift dress and flat sandals.

And it was not a designer handbag that was strapped to her shoulder.

From the way she held the sling, her burden seemed far more precious than that.

And then he saw her look down and smile and realised that she was holding a baby.

No!

He hauled himself back from the appalling assumption that the baby might be his and reminded himself that she had been a nanny once.

But she had told him how much she had hated it and had said she would never be a nanny again.

The baby was hers, Luka knew it, from the way she smiled down and caressed its head.

'No.'

He said it out loud this time and Amber looked up. 'Is everything okay?'

Luka didn't answer her, his mind was moving too fast.

It had been a year since he'd been with Cecelia.

Not quite to the day, although it would be soon.

And he remembered the very date of their parting.

Even the time.

It had been just after nine when she had left the building.

In fact, he recalled so many details.

Because life had got crazy since then, he told himself.

And life had just got a whole lot more complicated now.

'Pull over,' he instructed the driver. 'In fact, turn around.'

His driver did not point out that this busy street was not the place to execute a U-turn, and instead he complied.

Luka could feel the thump of his heart in his chest as he searched the pavement for another sight of her but she was nowhere to be seen.

His face remained impassive but his eyes scanned the crowd until he caught sight of her again and instructed his driver to pull over.

Safe from view behind tinted windows, he watched Cecelia.

She was certainly a touch slimmer than he remembered and, from what little he knew about pregnancy, if the baby was hers, shouldn't it be otherwise?

Luka took out his phone and the number he had considered calling far too many times was dialled now.

He watched as Cecelia reached for her phone.

'Hello?'

She would not know it was him, Luka realised, for after he had fired Sabine he'd had no choice but to change all his numbers.

'Cecelia.'

At the sound of his voice the world stopped.

The traffic, the noise, the shoppers on the busy street all faded to nothing at the sound of her name on his lips.

She knew instantly it was him, yet she did not reveal that. Instead, Cecelia played for time. 'Who's this?' she asked, and ran a nervous hand through her hair.

'Luka.'

'Oh.'

'Have I caught you at a bad time?'

'No, no, I'm just…' And he watched as she held the baby tighter to her, 'I'm actually on my lunch break.'

'Well, I need to speak with you. I was wondering if you could call by the office. There are a few issues we need to discuss.'

'Luka, I haven't worked for you in a year.'

'It's just a couple of accounting queries. Nothing serious but my accountant needs to verify a few things…' He wasn't even lying, because if indeed this was his baby there were certainly some things that needed to be discussed!

He was suddenly surprised that he hadn't already been fleeced.

'Can you come in?'

'I told you, I'm working.'

'After work,' Luka said. 'It won't take long. I'll have Marco stay back.'

'It's not terribly convenient.'

'Life isn't, is it?' he said, and ended the call.

She couldn't breathe.

In the middle of a packed London street she was as panicked as she had been on the day she had found out she was pregnant.

More so, for she hadn't loved her baby then.

He couldn't know about Pandora, Cecelia told herself.

No.

It must be work related.

Some document she hadn't signed or some expense that hadn't gone through.

After all, just last week she'd had to go into the diplomat's office and tie up a few loose ends.

Then, though, she had taken in Pandora.

She could hardly do the same with Luka.

Cecelia looked down at her tiny baby. The world was closing in and she knew she had to tell him.

Calmly.

She did not want Pandora to be exposed to any negative reaction, even if she was far too young to understand.

And for the very same reason, she would not be calling her aunt!

She arrived home all flustered, and of course Mrs Dawson wanted to stop for a chat.

'My daughter's just found out she's having twins!' Mrs Dawson said.

'How many grandchildren will that make?' Cecelia asked.

'Eight!' Mrs Dawson beamed. 'How's Pandora?'

'Wonderful,' Cecelia said, and watched as the old lady made Pandora smile.

'She's such a happy baby,' Mrs Dawson said. 'I never hear a peep.'

'Mrs Dawson…'

Cecelia loathed asking for help or being an imposition but she simply didn't know what else to do and Mrs Dawson had offered on several occasions.

'Could I ask you to look after Pandora for a couple of hours this afternoon?'

'I'd love to!'

'I'll pay you, of course.'

'You certainly won't. It will be my absolute pleasure.'

Why, oh, why could her aunt not have said that?

* * *

Cecelia dressed as if for an interview.

The navy suit was put on again for her visit to Kargas Holdings.

And even though she would only be gone for a couple of hours and Pandora had just been fed, she made up two bottles just in case. And her blanket and loads of nappies as well as Cecelia's phone number...

She was terribly nervous at the thought of leaving her, but Mrs Dawson was so friendly and seemed thrilled to have been asked.

'I really shan't be long,' Cecelia said. 'I just have to pop into work and I'll come straight back.'

'Pandora will be fine.'

And Pandora would be fine, Cecelia knew as she took the Tube.

But would *she* be?

Cecelia couldn't fathom what Luka's reaction might be, and she actually felt a little sick as she came out of the escalators and the building loomed up.

Cecelia could remember sitting in the café opposite and willing herself to go in and tell him.

She had no choice now.

The doorman smiled and then frowned and instead of waving her through she was told to go to Reception.

There a call was made and she stood with pink cheeks, feeling like one of his exes.

Which she was.

Sort of.

Finally, she received a visitor's pass and the code for the elevator.

Cecelia's hand was shaking as she punched in the numbers.

The air-conditioner should have been blissful, but

instead she could feel the sheen of perspiration on her face. She rubbed her palms on her skirt, just in case he decided to shake her hand.

As the elevator doors opened there was no Bridgette to greet her; instead, it was an unfamiliar woman who sat at Cecelia's old desk.

'I'll just let Luka know you're here,' she said. 'Perhaps you'd like to take a seat.'

'Actually, I think I'm seeing Marco. If you could let him know that I'm here...' She would get work out of the way and then she would speak with Luka, Cecelia decided.

'Marco?' She shook her head. 'He isn't in today.'

And then Cecelia heard Luka. 'I'll deal with this.'

For the first time in a year she felt his presence and she prickled all over at the sound of his voice.

Her head wanted to spin to face him but she resisted and instead slowly turned to him.

'Cecelia,' he greeted her.

'Luka.'

She had forgotten the absolute impact of him.

The year that had passed had dimmed him in a way she had not expected. His ruthlessness and playboy ways had been somewhat tempered by the memories of them in bed.

And he did not look in the least pleased to see her.

'Come through,' he said.

'But I thought I was seeing Marco.'

'I'm sure you soon will be,' Luka said as he led her through to his office. 'Please, take a seat.'

Cecelia was very glad to, for her legs felt as if they were made of rubber, and not just because she was nervous—yes, she had forgotten the absolute impact of him.

He looked incredible.

Gleaming was the word that came to mind.

His raven hair was worn shorter than she ever re-membered it being and it accentuated his sharp features. He was tanned, and although there had never been an ounce of spare flesh on him he now looked leaner.

Meaner, Cecelia thought, and her heart kicked into a gallop, though she did her level best not to show it.

Yes, being away from him for a year had certainly tempered Luka in her mind, for now she was back she remembered her despair at his reckless ways; the con-stant stream of women; his wealth and the power that came with that.

And he was her baby's father.

There had never been a doubt as to that, of course, but only now, back in his world, did it truly hit home.

He had essentially fired her on the last occasion she had been here. He had had her marched out of his life over the smallest slight.

Cecelia thought of his legal team and the constant battles they waged, for he would step over anyone to get a property he wanted.

And he was Pandora's father!

Cecelia did her best to meet Luka's eyes, which seemed no longer a velvet brown but as black as night as they appraised her. There was no hint of a smile on his mouth.

'Where are you working?' Luka asked.

'At the same place that I left here for,' Cecelia an-swered.

'You never did say where.'

'Didn't I?'

Oh, let the games begin, Luka thought.

He was turned on and enjoying the silent fight.

He watched her pink tongue run a nervous path along her lips. He looked at her cool green eyes and he fought not to walk right around that desk and shake the news from her.

He was certain the baby was his.

Why?

Because there had been no one else since that night.

Nearly a whole damn year—and not for the lack of options or opportunity.

And if he hadn't screwed his way out of the problem, then he was certain that neither had she.

Whatever had happened that night, or rather that morning, had taken a lot to get over.

He still hadn't.

And now he knew why—this morning he had found out he was a father.

But he had only found out by chance.

'How have you been, Cecelia?' he asked.

'You mean since I was marched out of the office?'

'Please,' he dismissed, 'you exaggerate.'

'How did Sabine work out?' Cecelia asked, remembering again the humiliation of that morning.

'She didn't,' he said. 'In fact, I *did* have *her* marched out of the office and I considered taking a restraining order out against her at one point.'

'Well, if you will insist on mixing business...' Cecelia started, but then she faltered. She just could not stand the thought of him with Sabine enough to pursue her line. 'Where's Bridgette?'

'She's on annual leave.'

Well, at least that sounded nice and normal.

'So what is it that you want to see me about?' Cecelia asked.

'There were a couple of expense forms that were flagged and Marco needed—'

'Could he not have emailed?'

'I guess,' Luka said, 'but I wanted to see you myself.'

She could not tell him now, Cecelia knew, for she simply couldn't make herself say it. She could barely look him in the eye, let alone tell him news that would turn his world upside down. Or maybe it wouldn't.

She needed to think this through properly, because Luka didn't play nice, she well knew it.

Luka Kargas had an entire legal team that worked on his behalf and if he decided she was the enemy then God help her.

Cecelia knew she must leave and go and get some proper advice and then she would tell him. 'Well, if you can have Marco email me when he's next in…' She picked up her bag. 'Anything else?'

'I'm not sure,' Luka said. 'Why don't we go and get dinner and catch up?'

'I don't think so.'

'A drink perhaps?'

'No.'

'It's been almost a year,' Luka said.

'How sweet that you remembered.' She gave a tight smile. 'You must celebrate a lot of one-night-stand anniversaries.' It looked like she could not do this without it descending into a row. 'Luka…' She stood. 'I'm going to go.'

The door looked a very long way off when Cecelia turned to face it. She had no idea the game he was playing but, whatever it was, she wanted out.

No way could she watch the anger flare in his features, for already the air was thick with tension.

But a tension she could not define.

Sex, with a dash of…

Cecelia didn't know what and she would not be staying to find out.

Her hand was on the handle of the door when he called to her.

'Have you forgotten something?' Luka asked.

Foolishly, she patted her bag. 'No.'

'I meant,' he said in a voice that was like a dagger wrapped in velvet, 'did you forget to tell me about my baby?'

The caress of his voice and then the knife to her back.

Her back was to him, but if there had been any doubt Luka knew now for certain that the baby was his, for her shoulders stiffened, followed by the slight buckle of her knees before she righted herself, although she still did not turn around.

'Sit down, Cecelia,' Luka said.

She did not follow orders any more.

Instead she stood there, trying to fathom how he knew. And, given that he did, Luka's reaction was the antithesis of anything she had expected. Cecelia had been sure that when she told him, the majority of any ensuing discussions would be convincing him that Pandora was his.

She was unprepared for this. Her reactions when around Luka were always extreme for he turned her from ordered to chaotic, and so, instead of turning around and calmly facing him, Cecelia wrenched open the door.

'Don't you dare walk off,' Luka warned in an ominous voice.

Except that was exactly what Cecelia did.

The was no one at her old desk and no one at Reception as she swiftly made her way through the vast space.

There was just the gleam of furniture and the scent of flowers in the air as she headed speedily for the lift.

She desperately wanted distance between them. She pressed the button for the lift, yet no light came on to indicate that it was on its way.

Cecelia pressed it again.

No, the lifts weren't out, she quickly realised, Luka must have changed the code! Usually it was altered to stop ex-lovers making their way up to him, never to prevent them from getting out!

Well, she'd take the fire escape, Cecelia decided, and turned angrily in time to see Luka calmly walking towards her.

'Come and sit down, Cecelia, and we will talk.'

'I'll take the stairs.'

'You can try.' Luka shrugged.

Cecelia knew he'd have no scruples about going after her and hauling her straight back.

'You can't keep me here, Luka,' she shouted. 'You had me come to the office under false pretences and you have no right—'

Oh, she knew she had said the wrong thing for even Cecelia stopped in mid-sentence as he walked towards her.

'Don't you dare speak to me about *rights* when you have denied me mine,' Luka warned, and he came so close that she shrank back against the cool wall of the elevator. 'Now you are to get back to my office so we can talk.'

'Luka…' she attempted. 'I was going to tell you.'

'I don't want to hear your lies and excuses,' he said. 'I don't care what you *might* have been going to do. I want to know about my child.'

'But I have to get back to her.'

She watched his jaw grit and the angry purse of his beautiful mouth as she realised that he had only just found out that their baby was a girl.

And Cecelia knew in that instant that she would never be forgiven for keeping Pandora from him.

'Luka, I know we have to talk and I understand that you're angry but I really can't do this now.'

'When then?' he demanded. 'On her eighteenth birthday? Or perhaps when your money has run out and you want to claim your meal ticket?'

'Luka, please.'

He watched as the ordered Cecelia put her hands to her ears.

'I can't row now.'

She was muddled, caught, confused.

And it wasn't just that he already knew.

The impact of being close to him again was an utter assault to her senses.

For the best part of a year she had fought not to think of him. Now that she faced him, worst of all, she was the liar and the guilty party.

'It's my first time away from her.'

A pathetic excuse perhaps, only it was the truth and it was killing her.

'Is she with your aunt?'

'God, no!' The words shot out and then she looked up at him. 'She's with my neighbour. Luka, I know we need to talk, I accept that, but it's not going to be wrapped up in an hour.'

'You clearly don't get it, Cecelia. Whatever the location, whatever the time, I shall be meeting my daughter tonight. You have denied me my rights for long enough.'

Cecelia had seen him like this before, though it had been in the workplace, and she knew Luka well enough to know that arguing would be futile. But aside from that, he was completely right—she had denied him his rights long enough.

'We can go to your home,' Luka said, 'or we can speak here or at mine, and then you take me to meet her or have her brought to me. But before you decide, know this, Cecelia. If you refuse to take me to my daughter, then the next contact we have shall be via a lawyer. I don't currently employ an expert in family law, but my team is already looking into it. Mess up again and the best shall be retained.' He saw her already pale skin go even paler but he felt no guilt. None at all. And he told her why. 'You started this, Cecelia.'

'Do you blame me?'

'Yes,' Luka swiftly answered. 'I blame you completely.'

CHAPTER TEN

CECELIA CHOSE HOME.

The drive to her flat had been a silent one. She had tried to speak once, to tell him his daughter's name, but he had told her to save it.

'If I want to know anything, I will ask.'

Right now, Luka had enough to process. He had a child. A girl.

He had been a father for three months and not known.

He could not deal with even one more piece of information that had been kept from him or he might just lose it.

Things would be at his pace from this point on and if Cecelia could take her time then so could he!

'I thought you said we needed to talk,' Cecelia pushed, wanting as much as possible out of the way before they got home.

'Well, I've changed my mind,' Luka said. 'It's too late for all that.'

Luka actually felt ill at the thought that anything could have happened to his daughter and he wouldn't have known.

He looked over at Cecelia, who sat opposite him, and he thought of the secret she had kept from him and that only by chance had he found out.

White hot was the rage that seared through Luka and he was doing his level best to contain it.

'We're here,' Cecelia said as his driver pulled up close to the main door to her flat. But as the driver came round and opened the door, Luka didn't immediately get out.

Luka, who could face anything, was for the first time nervous at the prospect of what lay ahead, for in a moment he would meet his daughter for the first time.

'Aren't you coming in?' Cecelia asked.

'Of course I am.' Luka shot Cecelia a look of contempt. 'I'm hardly going to meet her in the street.'

She could feel his loathing as he entered her small flat. She hadn't noticed how messy it was when she had headed out.

Cecelia noticed now.

The ordered world she had once inhabited, one where she put out her clothes for the next morning the night before, had long since gone. The tiny bundle that she had birthed meant that she lurched from one feed to the next and grabbed a quick shower and a scrape of her comb through her hair in the short bursts when Pandora slept.

Cecelia did not attempt a rapid tidy.

Instead, she glanced at the magazines on the coffee table to distract her anxious thoughts. There were some colic drops too and a couple of mugs, and some baby blankets strewn across the sofa—the aftermath of a difficult night.

It had been a difficult, yet wonderful three months.

She was permanently exhausted and lonely too. She was barely speaking with her aunt and uncle and she was not exactly inundated with friends. The few Cecelia had were either single or child-free by choice. There had been cards, flowers and visits when Pandora had first

been born, but, understandably they did not want their
Sunday brunches pierced by a baby's cries and Cecelia
didn't have space in her brain for decent conversation.

She was a mother.

A new one.

Yet she had a three-month head start on Luka.

'Would you like…?' Cecelia started but Luka wasn't
here for a chat and neither would he be taking a seat.

'Could you fetch my daughter, please?'

'Of course.'

Mrs Dawson was nosy enough that she would have
seen the expensive car pull up and know that Cecelia
had a guest, and so she didn't invite her in for a chat.

'She was as good as gold,' Mrs Dawson said, as she
handed Pandora over. 'Fell asleep in my arms.'

'Thank you so much.'

'And she's just been fed,' Mrs Dawson said as she
collected up her things.

Pandora was wrapped in a soft lilac blanket and Cecelia held her close and inhaled the delicious baby scent.
Oh, yes, her tiny world was changing and Cecelia did
not want to let her go. Having thanked Mrs Dawson,
she headed across the hall but Pandora picked up on her
tension and started to cry.

Good, Cecelia thought, even as she moved to hush
her. *Let him see how it really is. Tell me off, write your
cheque and be gone.* For she could not deal with the
thought of handing Pandora over to him. And, no, she
did not want her daughter spending weekends and holidays with a father who partied just as hard as he worked.

As she stepped into the lounge he was there waiting, so tailored and exquisite and with angry black eyes.
She could not believe that Luka was really in her home.

He did not belong here.

Luka belonged in his office castle or creating merry hell aboard his yacht.

The expensive scent, the stunning suit all felt like too much to process right now.

Her child's father was a reckless playboy, and in her arms she held the consequence of their one night together.

She soothed Pandora as Luka stood watching but he made no move to come over. 'I really was going to tell you,' she told him.

'Then why didn't you when I called you earlier today?'

'I was standing in the street!'

He heard the urgent sincerity in her voice and for the first time today he knew she was telling the truth. Cecelia did not know he had been watching her when she had taken the call.

Still, the grain of honesty from her barely appeased him for it accounted only for a few seconds of the past year.

'Why didn't you say anything back in the office?' he asked as he gazed at the bundle she held in her arms. Really he could see only the blanket and he was playing for time, nervous now to meet her.

'I couldn't do it face to face.' Another truth, not that he believed her, Cecelia could see. 'I tried to call you a couple of times during the pregnancy. I couldn't get through.'

'You didn't try very hard.'

'No,' she admitted.

'Why?'

That she couldn't really answer but she tried. 'I was scared of your reaction. I thought you'd tell me to get rid of her, or say that I'd tried to trap you by getting pregnant...'

'I was there that morning, Cecelia. I do know how babies are made and that it takes two.'

It was the closest she had come to a smile since facing him again, but Luka did not see it. He had no interest in the past right now, for in that second the small blanket slipped a little and he saw a shock of dark hair and a pale cheek and suddenly he forgot how to breathe. There in his chest it felt as if an iron fist had sunk in.

He walked over and Cecelia felt him enter her space—only it had nothing to do with her, simply the infant she held in her arms.

She watched one, long, olive finger come and tenderly stroke the little baby's cheek. 'Can I hold her?'

'She's a bit unsettled...'

'I was only asking, to be polite,' Luka said, and now he no longer asked—he told her instead in a voice that was calm but the words hit like sleet. *'Give my baby to me.'*

She handed Pandora to him and he took her into his arms, more skilfully than she had predicted—because, of course, she had imagined how her baby would look in his arms. She watched him cradle his daughter and carefully take a seat on the couch as his eyes never left Pandora's face.

'What name did *you* choose for her?' he asked, and Cecelia heard the scold in his tone.

He would change it if he did not like it, Luka decided.

How dared she take such an important choice from him?

There were tears at the back of her nose and throat and she had to swallow before she could respond. 'Pandora.'

But he would not be changing it, for the second he heard the name Luka loved it.

It meant 'all gifts', which indeed she was, and it was Greek and…

He let out a soft, yet not quite mirthless laugh. He had decided a caustic response was his to make, yet none came, for the name was completely perfect as for the first time Pandora opened her eyes to look at him.

They were navy and surrounded by spiky black lashes and she simply stared up at her father and met his gaze.

Luka pushed back the pale blanket to reveal more dark hair and he looked at her pretty rosebud mouth. For the first time in his life he felt the threat of tears.

Luka had never held a baby, let alone thought he might father one.

Now he held a daughter he had only found out existed today. His free hand held hers, looking at the slender fingers and tiny nails. Then he traced her eyebrows and imprinted her beauty on his mind—her little mouth and the soft pink of her skin—and when she stared back at him with sleepy navy eyes Pandora gave him a smile.

Her eyelashes seemed too heavy and he watched as she closed her eyes in sleep and he simply breathed in the baby scent of her and the miracle of her existence.

And had her mother got her way, Luka would never have known she was here.

Any tenderness left his eyes as he looked up at Cecelia. 'Pandora indeed,' Luka said. 'However, your secret is out now.'

'I really was going to tell you—'

'Save it.'

'Honestly Luka, when I first found out—'

'Save it,' he said again. 'I won't have this moment marred by your lies and I won't have this discussion in front of our child.' Then he looked down at Pandora. 'Perhaps it is time to put her down.'

He stood and Cecelia nodded and held out her arms to take Pandora but Luka did not simply hand her over. 'I can take her to the nursery.'

'Nursery!' She let out a wry laugh. 'Luka, it's a one-bedroomed flat, not a penthouse apartment.'

While true, there was a small study that could be turned into a nursery in the future, but for now Pandora had been sleeping in with her. Cecelia could not bear the thought of her daughter waking up and crying in the dark alone.

Luka handed over Pandora but Cecelia would not, or could not, meet his eyes. She just held her daughter close to her and headed for the bedroom.

She knew he was furious.

Cecelia was furious with herself.

She should have told him at the very least in his office but she had panicked.

Now she had no one to blame but herself for the situation she found herself in.

Cecelia put Pandora down. Unlike last night, when she had protested every time she had been lowered to the mattress, now Pandora made not a sound.

She stared at her for a moment, aware that Luka stood in the doorway, watching them.

He wanted to know his daughter's routines and things like how to put a tiny baby to sleep. All of this was completely alien to him.

He saw that Cecelia covered her with a blanket and then kissed her fingers and placed them on the baby's head before turning to leave the bedroom.

'I don't want to argue…' Cecelia said as she walked past him.

They moved into the hallway and she awaited the interrogation, but instead it seemed he was about to leave.

'You're going?' Cecelia checked, not really believing that was it, but he was heading for the front door.

'Yes, it has been a long day,' Luka said. 'I just returned from Greece this morning.'

He had been on his way back from the airport when he had seen her.

It felt like a lifetime ago.

'I was there for my father's funeral.'

It was as if the carpet beneath her feet had turned into a flying one, for she felt the jolt of the ground and the world tip off kilter.

She had known she would never be forgiven by Luka, but what he had just revealed told her that it was a certain fact now.

His father had died without knowing he had a granddaughter.

'I'm sorry,' Cecelia attempted.

'Oh, no, you're not,' Luka said. 'How could you be when you did not know him?'

She looked into his eyes, which were not entirely unreadable for she could see the loathing there.

'When do you want to see her again?' Cecelia attempted.

'Tomorrow,' Luka responded crisply. 'A car will be here for you at nine in the morning.'

'A car?' Cecelia checked. 'Am I to bring her to you or?'

'I am taking Pandora to Xanero tomorrow. Naturally, I would like my mother to meet her granddaughter.'

'Luka, no...' She reached and caught his arm but he shook her hand off as if he could not bear the slightest touch from her. 'She's not ready to travel.'

'Why ever not?' he demanded.

'She doesn't have a passport.'

'I have a contact at the embassy and an urgent one can be arranged on our way to the airport.'

'No! She's not ready.'

'Pandora is three months old and shall be travelling on my private jet accompanied by her mother. I don't see any issue.'

'I might have plans tomorrow,' Cecelia attempted. To no avail.

'Then cancel them.'

'Luka, I'm not trying to keep you from her. You can see Pandora tomorrow, of course you can, but you can't just walk in here and tell me that tomorrow I have to leave for Greece...'

'Are you quite sure about that?' Luka checked. 'Because the way I see it, tomorrow you can either get on a plane and head to a luxurious resort for a week...'

'A week?' Cecelia gulped.

He nodded. 'There you shall be catered for and beautifully looked after. Once there, the best nannies will be available to assist as I get to know my daughter and her grandmother meets her.' He frowned as if bemused by Cecelia. 'I thought you would jump at the chance.'

'No!'

'So you would rather spend the next few days in court? When the outcome will be the same—Pandora will be coming to Xanero, my lawyers will see to that.'

She felt sick.

It was like David and Goliath, except she wasn't the good guy here and the courts might well agree.

She would be portrayed as the bitch who had kept him from his child, up against the might of Luka Kargas.

She had lost already, Cecelia knew as she watched

him walk down the small garden path, brushing against weeds and neglected overgrown bushes because for the past months gardening had been the furthest thing from her mind.

'I'll see you tomorrow!' he called. 'Be ready.'

And even if Luka was in no mood to speak, even if she had no right to an answer, Cecelia did have a question.

'How did you know?' she called out to the dark and watched him halt. She was not asking how he had known about the baby; she was asking how he had been so certain that Pandora was his.

'How did I know?' Luka checked exactly what she was asking as he turned around. 'Are you going to try and drag things out with a DNA test to keep her from me even longer?'

'Of course not. But most men would demand one. I'm just asking why you're so certain…' Her voice trailed off as he walked back toward her, and then he came and stood closer to her than he had all evening.

So close that she could feel his breath on her cheek as he answered the question.

'I know, Cecelia, because when your legs were wrapped tight around me…' She was dizzy from lack of oxygen and she could feel his breath warm her cheek as he painted a vivid picture. 'When I screwed you slow and deep and came inside you,' he continued and her neck was rigid and her eyes screwed closed as he taunted her with the vision of them, 'you may recall that I was unsheathed.'

'Luka…' She begged with a single word that he stop. He did not.

'And given how long it took to get inside you, I doubt you went from my bed straight to someone else's. And,' he continued, 'given your abhorrence that we did not use protection, I would guess that lapse was as rare for you as it was for me.'

His voice was a taunt, both sensual and cruel as he took her back to that night. 'That is how I know,' he said, and then the thick, rich voice stopped and he pulled back and looked at her face, flushed in the porch light, confusion darting in her eyes.

He confused her, he excited her and made her want to sink to her knees and run, all at the same time.

But then he made things abundantly clear.

'We were so hot, Cecelia, and we could have been good, but you chose to walk away. You left. And then you denied me the knowledge of my child and I hate you for that.' And then, when she'd already got the dark message, he gave it a second coat and painted it black. 'I absolutely hate you.'

'No mixed messages, then?' She somehow managed a quip but there was nothing that could lighten this moment.

'Not one. Let me make things very clear. I am not taking you to Greece to get to know you better, or to see if there is any chance for us, because there isn't. I want no further part of you. The fact is, you are my daughter's mother and she is too young to be apart from you. That won't be the case in the near future.'

'How near?'

Fear licked the sides of her heart.

'I don't know.' He shrugged. 'I know nothing about babies, save what I have found out today. But I learn fast,' he said, 'and I will employ only the best so very soon, during my access times, Pandora and I will do just fine without you.'

'Luka, please…' She could not stand the thought of

being away from Pandora and she was spinning at the thought of taking her daughter to Greece, but Luka was done.

'I'm going, Cecelia,' Luka said. 'I have nothing left to say to you.'

That wasn't quite true, for he had one question.

'Did you know you were pregnant when you left?' Luka asked.

'I had an idea…'

'The truth, Cecelia.'

And she ached now for the days when he had been less on guard and had called her Cece, even though it had grated so much at the time.

And now it was time to be honest and admit she had known she was pregnant when she had left. 'Yes.'

'But,' Luka pointed out, 'given we hadn't slept together then, your resignation had nothing to do with the pregnancy.'

That was another part that stung, Luka thought as his driver opened the door to his car—she'd been leaving already.

CHAPTER ELEVEN

SILENCE WAS CRUEL.

Where once there would have been conversation…
where once he had annoyed her by shortening her
name…now that delicious voice was no longer aimed
at her.

As promised, a car arrived at nine but, rather than
Luka, it was his latest PA who got out. She introduced
herself as Amber and gave Cecelia a very efficient
smile when she raised a question and assured her that
of course there was a baby seat in the car.

The driver dealt with her bags but Luka barely
looked up when she strapped in Pandora.

He was wearing khaki linen pants and a black T-
shirt—more casually dressed than she had ever seen
him—yet he certainly cut a dash. He was wearing
shades and looked very sullen, and only when Pandora was safely strapped in did he acknowledge them.

Cecelia got a brief nod.

For Pandora, he took off his shades and she got the
benefit of his full smile, a kiss on the forehead and the
warmth of his voice.

Cecelia watched as Pandora smiled and cooed up at
him and seemed to know him already.

He looked tired, Cecelia noted.

Beautiful, but very tired and she thought of the past few days he must have had, with his father dying and finding out that he had a daughter. Yet he turned on the smiles for Pandora. She had never thought this side to Luka existed, but then again she too had fallen in love with Pandora at first sight.

As they were driven to the embassy, the incredibly efficient Amber addressed Cecelia.

'The accommodation has all been arranged but anything that you or Pandora need, please just make me aware.'

Cecelia gave a curt nod.

That used to be her world, Cecelia thought—taking care of Luka's ex-lovers and all the ensuing dramas their trysts had created.

Admittedly, she hadn't been in Amber's situation, sorting out the sudden news that her boss had a baby, but Amber was handling the situation as if it happened every day.

Oh, please let him not have slept with her, Cecelia thought as Amber carried on with her questions. 'The chef has asked if there are any food issues or allergies?'

'No.' Cecelia shook her head, then tried to soften her terse response. 'I can eat anything…'

But that wasn't what Amber had been asking—'I meant are there any allergies or issues with Pandora?'

She glanced over at Luka, who was staring out of the window. She saw the ghost of a smile on his lips as she was put in her place.

This wasn't about the mother!

'Pandora drinks formula,' Cecelia tartly responded. 'I hardly need a gourmet chef to prepare her bottles.'

'Well, I do,' Luka said, and turned to look right at

her. 'So, please answer the questions correctly. From this day forward I need to know such things.'

Cecelia briefly closed her eyes. 'No,' she answered. 'Pandora has no allergies that I know of.'

'Good,' he said, and then got back to looking out of the window.

The embassy was efficient.

The flight was, for Cecelia, an emotional hell.

There was seemingly no strained atmosphere on his part, for he simply carried on as if she were not there.

His jet was luxurious and Cecelia knew it well, though it felt very different today. Instead of joining Luka at the table for a meal and talking work, once Pandora had been fed and settled, her meal was served in an area to the rear of the lounge.

The food was no doubt sublime, but Cecelia, who had earlier said she'd eat anything, just pushed it around her plate. She felt awkward as she dined alone while Luka and Amber sat at the table and went through the sudden changes to his schedule.

That used to be me, Cecelia thought.

Her old life seemed a very long way off right now. So much was different, but how she felt about Luka remained.

All she had put on hold by leaving, all she had attempted to erase by distance, had come flooding back.

Quite simply, Luka Kargas was as devastatingly stunning to Cecelia as he had been the day they had met.

Motherhood had changed an awful lot of things, but it seemed it hadn't changed that one thing in the slightest.

With the meals cleared away, Cecelia dozed, one ear trained to listen out for Pandora.

Amber was busy on the computer and, though tired, Luka knew he was too wired to sleep.

He walked over to the bassinet and looked at the daughter he had met just yesterday.

Pandora was perfection.

Her tiny nails were trim and neat as her fingers closed around his. And she wore a little white cotton baby suit dotted with daisies.

And then he looked over at her mother and this time his face did not harden.

Cecelia wore a grey linen dress that was rather crumpled, and he noticed her once immaculate hair needed a cut. There were grey smudges beneath her eyes and even her lips were too pale.

It was as if all Cece's colour, all her energy had drained into Pandora and the anger in him dimmed a notch when he thought of all she must have been through.

And then she must have felt him watching her, for Cecelia opened her eyes and met his.

'Why don't you go and lie down?' Luka suggested.

'Pandora's due to wake soon.'

'I'll be here.'

She felt dismissed as she was shown to a cabin, though it was utter bliss to lie down after a night spent frantically packing for Xanero.

A light touch to her arm jolted Cecelia awake. She got up from the bed and headed to the main cabin for the final descent into Xanero.

Thanks to rather too many searches on the Internet as she'd attempted to put together the mystery of him, Cecelia actually recognised the island from the air. She saw white Orthodox churches with their round domes, and the sprawling whitewashed buildings that gleamed against the backdrop of an azure Mediterranean.

They landed behind the sprawling complex and were driven in air-conditioned comfort to the villa that would be her home for the next week.

Luka got out and it was he who held Pandora as he pushed open a large cobalt-blue door and stood back as Cecelia stepped in.

It was stunning, with mosaic-tiled floors, huge couches and an endless view of the ocean, but she could not take it all in with Luka there.

'I'll be fine.'

'I want to check you have everything you need for Pandora.'

There was everything she could possibly need and a whole lot more should she possibly want it. She even had her own pool, Cecelia noticed as she looked out. Then she thought of Luka and his start in life and there was both jealousy and anger combined as she thought of him chatting up women.

Of course she said nothing, just remained quiet as he showed her around, until they came to what was clearly a nursery.

There was a room with white organza fluttering in the windows and a heavy dark wooden crib made up in white bedlinen. There was a little intercom on a table, and it was a long way off from the main suite.

'Pandora sleeps in with me.'

'I have had an identical room made up in my villa,' Luka said. 'The nanny suggested that it might help for her surroundings to be familiar when Pandora is with me.'

Yes, it made perfect sense, but she felt with her heart,

not her head. 'I would like her crib moved through to my room.'

'As you wish,' Luka said.

'And she's too young to be away from me overnight.'

'You're not breastfeeding,' he pointed out.

'Another black mark…'

'Oh, grow up,' he retorted.

'Luka, I don't want her waking up in the night and me not being there.' She was starting to panic, and that was something she did not want Luka to see, but she could remember waking up and calling out for her mother in the night and she would not put Pandora through the same. 'I am not having her apart from me.'

'You worry about a night spent away from your daughter, yet your silence sentenced me to three months without her. You denied me the chance to plan for her, or see my child when she was born…so don't start complaining about one night. Cecelia, it is time to get used to the fact that I am her father and I'm not going anywhere.'

He saw her throat tighten as she swallowed and caught her rapid blink and then watched as Cecelia sat down.

'Are you okay?'

'I'm just warm…'

He frowned because it was shady and cool in here and the journey had certainly been a comfortable one.

'I was up all night, packing, trying to make sure I had everything…'

'I told you that I would take care of all that.'

'Well, I'm not very used to…'

Cecelia stopped.

She was rather too used to having to take care of everything and could not quite get her head around the fact there was now someone else.

It both unsettled her and comforted her.

The decisions regarding Pandora felt so huge at times. Even giving up the breast for a bottle had been angst-ridden.

Never had she imagined that had Luka known about Pandora she might have been able to discuss it with him.

It wasn't the heat that had unsettled her, or exhaustion.

His words had hit like shrapnel buried deep and she sat there as he poured some iced water and then handed it to her.

Yet she could not think about how his words had effected her now.

'I guessed you wouldn't have time for shopping so Amber is sorting you out a wardrobe...'

'I can dress myself, Luka.'

'Well, there's not much call for navy suits here...'

It was a dig at her staid wardrobe.

'You don't know me out of work.'

'Oh, but I can guess.'

He was right.

Cecelia had sat on her bedroom floor with her suitcase last night and known that the truth was she had nothing to pack for a holiday.

Not really.

But then he surprised her.

'I apologise,' Luka said suddenly. 'That was uncalled-for. How you dress is your concern.'

It was a rather backhanded apology and she gave a small mirthless laugh.

'I've lost weight since last year,' Cecelia said. 'And finding a capsule wardrobe so I can swan off to Greece at a moment's notice hasn't exactly been high on my list of priorities.'

'Then it's lucky that it's being taken care of,' he said, and she nodded. 'Is there anything else you need?'

'No.'

'There is a spa and a salon. You don't need an appointment. I have told them to accommodate you whenever you so choose. And there is the restaurant and a table reserved solely for you for the duration of your stay. Naturally, if you would prefer to dine here, just say.'

Cecelia nodded.

'When she wakes up, if you call the number by the phone you will be put through to the nanny, who will come and fetch Pandora.'

'How can you have arranged a nanny so quickly? Luka, I'm not just handing her over to someone you've hired in a rush...'

'There are several nannies at this resort and, given the clientele, we hire only the best. The best of the best shall be caring for my daughter. Her name is Roula and she has worked here for more than five years and was once the private nanny to royalty. You didn't check with me before you left her with a neighbour, and I did not question that choice either. I assume you want the best for her. Please afford me the same courtesy and never again suggest that I don't have my daughter's interests at heart.'

He gave the sleeping Pandora a light kiss and handed her over before striding off. Cecelia sat there, holding her daughter, his words playing over and over in her head.

I'm not going anywhere.

They were words she had never expected to hear, and she was scared to believe them.

Fair enough, he was angry now about being kept in

the dark, but when that anger had faded, when Pandora was teething and screaming deep in the night…

Yes, it felt like shrapnel was making its way to the surface as she recalled the fear of waking up in a house with no one there.

Pushing open her mother's bedroom door and seeing the empty bed.

Creeping downstairs, ears straining for the sound of chatter and laughter and bracing herself to be scolded for disturbing the grown-ups.

But no one had been there.

She had never known when her mother would be back, and then one day she hadn't been. Cecelia held her daughter tight and swore she would never know the same.

Cecelia jumped as the sound of a soft bell reverberated through the villa.

At the door stood Amber and two porters, along with another woman who was sultry looking and wore a sarong.

'Luka said you wouldn't have time to pack,' Amber said as she breezed in with the porters, who carried a whole lot of designer bags. 'They won't be long…'

She was mildly grateful to Luka for the excuse he had given Amber.

'And this is Roula.' Amber introduced them. 'The nanny.'

Oh, my!

When Luka had said she'd been a nanny for royalty, somehow Cecelia had imagined a crisp white dress and big black rubber shoes.

Instead, the nanny was barefoot and stunning.

'Luka suggested that I come over and meet you,' Roula said. 'You can tell me your daughter's ways and anything I need to know and hopefully meeting me will make things easier on you.'

It would be easier if she wasn't so stunning.

Pandora woke up and smiled when Roula first met her and didn't cry when she was held.

'Sophie—Luka's mother—is so excited to meet her,' Roula said. 'After such a sad loss there is sunshine again.'

There was no more putting it off, and all too soon she watched as the gorgeous Roula headed off with her daughter.

And it hurt.

Not just that they were apart, more that there was a grandmother excited to meet Pandora, a family gathering taking place from which she was excluded.

After they had gone, she opened the huge dark wooden dresser to see what clothes had been chosen for her and glimpsed an array of terribly sexy one-piece swimming suits cut high in the leg with plunging backs.

She did not belong in this world.

There was a rose-gold bikini that Cecelia held for a moment, though could never imagine putting on, and she realised that there was colour now lining her wardrobe.

There was a rose-gold silk dress too, in the same fabric as the bikini, a sensual throw-on for when you dined by the pool, Cecelia guessed.

And there were fragrances and oils by the bath.

Heaven knew, she needed them.

Her habits had long since slipped by the wayside. First to go had been her routine foils and so now her hair was back to its original strawberry blonde, with some rather long dry ends.

And she had long since stopped straightening it.

So much for looking sleek and together when she faced him and told him about Pandora.

Instead he had found out on his own.

And now, here in Xanero, she faced his wrath.

CHAPTER TWELVE

PARADISE WAS LONELY without him.

She called for lunch and ate in the villa and then, after a doze, she put on the most modest of the swimming costumes, took a book outside and read by the pool.

The book didn't pull her in, though.

All too often Cecelia found herself looking up and thinking of Luka and his misspent youth.

And so she gave in, tied on a sarong and went for a walk along Luka's private beach.

The Mediterranean shimmered like an endless sapphire and the white sand was pristine, but there was no solace there either.

For Luka's yacht was moored in the distance and she thought of the morning he had invited her to join him.

As his plaything.

They were poles apart yet eternally joined by a daughter they clearly both loved.

She had thought she'd known hell before.

Working alongside him, while loving him had been torture.

But this was worse. It did not cease at the end of the working day and there would be no annual leave.

Instead, this was her future.

He was now a permanent part of her life.

So far, he hadn't put a foot wrong, but soon she would have to deal with the glamorous beauties and his tawdry social life.

Some time soon, Cecelia was sure of it, there would be his latest long-limbed beauty lying on the sun lounger, or splashing in the water beside him with *her* daughter.

And there was no escape from that.

Pandora would talk one day and no doubt she would hear about daddy's new friends.

So Cecelia returned to the poolside to brood and that was how he found her.

She was huddled under the shade as if the sun might bite and the pool and poolside were pristine from lack of use. She startled when she looked up and saw him.

He wore only bathers and carried Pandora with a muslin cloth over her. She was asleep against his chest.

And she wore only a nappy.

'Pandora should be covered in the sun…' Cecelia chastised.

'And she is,' Luka pointed out. 'She fell asleep on the walk over here. Shall I put her down?'

Cecelia nodded and held open the door to the villa. His hair was wet and she knew he'd been in the pool.

'You didn't have Pandora by the pool, did you?' Cecelia checked.

'Of course I did, but we were always in the shade and she loved the water.'

'You took her in!' There was horror in her voice as she followed him through the villa. 'Luka, she's far too young.'

'Pandora adored it.'

She was appalled—in fact, Cecelia was furious, but she held her tongue as he tenderly lowered his daughter.

Pandora was clearly exhausted.

She barely stirred as he lightly covered her with the muslin, and as Luka walked off he tried not to glance at the large bed, or Cecelia's rumpled dress flung over the chair.

And a pile of bikinis that she'd clearly tried on and discarded.

He kept having to remind himself how furious he was, yet this woman was a constant turn-on.

Out of her bedroom, he headed to the fridge and pulled out a bottle of wine and selected two glasses.

'This is my villa,' Cecelia pointed out, not liking his bold intrusion.

'Okay, you serve, then,' he said, and handed her the bottle and glasses. 'I'll be outside.'

God, he was arrogant, Cecelia thought, and spent five minutes trying to find a corkscrew before she worked out it was a screw top.

Her temper was still bubbling, and yet it was clear he was here to talk. Well, as long as he was prepared to listen too because there was no way he was taking Pandora in the pool again.

She walked outside but it wasn't the glare of the sun that had her momentarily close her eyes.

It was his beauty.

Practically naked, except for black trunks slung low on his hips, he lay on a lounger.

He had a restless energy to him that she recognised from a year of working alongside him, and she felt a flutter of nerves low in her stomach as she approached.

She poured him a glass of wine and sparkling water for herself and then she suppressed a smile at his *You serve, then* comment.

'Here,' she said, and handed him the glass. 'Luka, we need to talk about Pandora...'

'I know we do and it's the only reason I'm here,' he said, more to remind himself, for he was on slow boil for Cece—or Cecelia as he would remember to call her now.

'How was your mother with her?'

'They got on wonderfully. She's thrilled to have a granddaughter...' He kept trying to be angry, but the truth was, it felt as if there was less and less to be angry about. 'She is concerned for you, and all that you must have been through alone.'

'Oh.'

Luka was too.

But there was something else concerning him and it was something that urgently needed to be discussed.

'I've been speaking with my PR people in the UK and it would seem that there is a lot of press interest in me at the moment.'

Cecelia felt her heart sink.

'With my father's death and the new hotels...' He didn't bother to explain it all but Cecelia got the gist.

The press would love to get their hands on the billionaire playboy now a father.

He read her concern. 'It is secure here, that I can assure you. Nobody can get a photo while you are in the complex, I took care of that long ago. The only risky place is my yacht.'

'Well, I shan't be going there!' She gave a tight smile. 'But, even so, I can't be expected to stay behind the wall...'

'Firstly, it is hardly a prison complex. There are miles of walks and you have access to my private beach. You are hardly going to be confined to four walls. You can take Pandora for a walk in the village if you feel you want to get out. I doubt a mother and baby will raise much interest.'

'I mean, if she's seen with you. Oh, God!' She stood and looked out to sea as if a thousand cameras were trained on them.

'I've already told you that the hotel and grounds are secure and I won't be joining you on any strolls.'

She felt heat flood her cheeks as again he placed distance between them and she tried to quickly change tack. 'I meant in London.'

'For now, I shall see Pandora here.' He saw the small frown form between her eyes. 'You just said you don't want any photos taken.'

'But if you're going to be in her life, how can you avoid her while in London?'

'I'm not avoiding Pandora,' Luka said, and then he put things bluntly. 'I'm going to be avoiding her mother.'

'If you want to be in her life, then that's going to prove rather difficult.'

'Amber is going through my schedule and for now, one week a month I am arranging things so that I shall be working from here.'

'But you have a home in London and you can't ask me to upend my life!'

'Hold on right there. Had you done the right thing in the first place, we would have had time to organise things better. Had you bothered to tell me I was soon to be a father I might have been able to sort my schedule better. Had you—'

'I get it,' Cecelia said, and held up her hand to halt him.

'I don't think you do,' Luka said. 'I don't believe for a moment you were going to tell me. I cannot believe I could have gone through my entire life not knowing about Pandora. She's my *daughter*...' he said. She heard the throaty rasp in his voice and she knew then how badly it was hurting him.

'Luka, I thought you would tell me to take care of things.'

'You assumed an awful lot.'

'My father asked my mother to.'

'She told you that?'

'No, the one time I met him he was shouting at her, telling her that he'd given her money for a termination. I didn't know what it meant, of course, until I looked it up.'

'I would never have asked that.'

'What would you have said then?' she flared.

'I don't know...'

'Well, neither did I!' Cecelia said, and she fought to keep herself from shouting.

'But I would have taken care of you and I would have ensured the best of care for the birth. And I would have been there when she was born and held her. And who knows what would have happened between us, but you denied us any chance of finding that out.'

Yes, he was angry.

But, yes, he understood better.

'You should have trusted me enough to tell me.'

'Trusted you! With the reckless way you live your life and your disposable attitude to women?'

'They don't have an issue with it,' Luka said. 'Well, most don't. I deliberately choose women who know what they want and are more than happy to indulge in a good time.' He could see the burn on her cheeks and he turned the knife. 'Women who don't wake up with regret...'

'Women who paid you.'

'Do you know what, Cecelia, you used to be a turn-on but I'm sick of the constant disapproval in your eyes.'

But, oh, it wasn't disapproval in her eyes, it was jealousy and it was want—not that she told him that, and so Luka spoke on.

'You're so busy being the perfect parent and before that the perfect PA you don't even know how to have fun.'

'Yes, I do.'

'You haven't even been in the pool!'

'You don't get to dictate what I do with my time,' Cecelia snapped. 'And about the pool, I don't want Pandora in the water...'

'Roula is a trained swimming instructor and, given that Pandora's going to be spending a lot of time surrounded by water, it seems prudent to teach her to swim.'

'She's three months old!'

'And she swam straight to the top.'

'Are you telling me you threw her in?'

'Roula and I were in the water with her.'

She felt ill at the thought of Pandora in the water and sick too at the thought of him and Roula, sharing that time with her baby.

'I want Pandora back home,' Cecelia said. 'This is too much. Luka, I want her back in London.'

'Tough!' Luka said. 'One week a month you are going to be here, and you can mope around and check for photographers or you can live a little.'

She incensed him, she really did.

He thought of that body of hers that never saw the sun and he did the only thing he could think of in response. He threw her up over his shoulder and carried her to the pool.

'Luka!'

Cecelia was raging and furious, not that it stopped him.
He just dropped her right into the deep end.

She flailed for a moment and then came up, and as she did, she heard another splash.

Luka.

He was there as she surfaced, spluttering and furious and swimming straight for the edge, but he caught her and held her at the waist as it was too deep to reach the bottom of the pool.

'How dare you!' she shouted.

'Have you never been thrown in the water before?'

'Of course not.'

'And do you know how to swim?'

'Of course I do.'

But it was nice, so nice to be in the water and facing him, nice to feel his hands strong on her waist and the sun beating on her shoulders.

Nice to know that her baby was doing things that she had never even dreamed of as a child and that she had a father who adored her.

And it was also scary to be under his spell again.

To know, from the ragged edge to his breathing, that he was turned on and to know from the warmth spreading through her that she was turned on too.

And to know that right now she could wrap her legs around him and be lost to Luka again.

But would it be *Bored on Monday so we might as well do it* sex for him? Cecelia pondered as she gazed into dark eyes.

Yes, she decided, because that was how he lived.

And so she disengaged from him and hauled herself from the water.

She was here as Pandora's mother.

That was all.

CHAPTER THIRTEEN

CECELIA WOKE EARLY.

Only not to the familiar cries of Pandora.

Silence really was cruel for she had been locked in a dream where Luka's kiss did not end and with an ache and heat low in her legs, and a body that throbbed for him.

She forced her eyes open and pulled herself out of bed and then went to check on Pandora.

She was asleep on her back with her little arms up above her head, as if cheering.

They had been here for almost a week and they were starting to get into a gentle routine.

The mornings were for her and Pandora alone, but around eleven Roula would come over and fetch her. Luka would take a long lunch break and spend time with her along with her *yia-yia*—her grandmother—who doted on her apparently.

Late afternoon, after her nap, Pandora would return to Cecelia.

And it was nice.

Cecelia was starting to relax into it and had, after her impromptu dip in the pool, started to swim each day and take regular walks along Luka's private beach.

It was a long stretch of cove that made for a perfect

walk, splashing through the breaking waves and breathing in the fresh sea air.

On her final full day in Xanero before she and Pandora flew home tomorrow, it wasn't by coincidence that Luka headed down to the beach to join her.

It still galled him that she had kept the news of the pregnancy from him, but he understood better why she had.

He wasn't exactly fatherhood material.

Or he hadn't been.

And he wasn't exactly a family man.

Yet he wanted to be.

He was still infatuated with Cecelia, and his desire for her had never gone, though he knew he must not rush things.

Even so, tomorrow she left for London. Three more weeks apart, and not just apart from his daughter.

He ached for Cecelia. He ached for the glimpse of the smile he sometimes prised from her reluctant lips, and for the way she sometimes made him laugh.

'Hey,' Luka said, and he saw that he had startled her.

'Where's Pandora?'

'Being spoiled,' he said. 'My mother wondered if you would like to join her for breakfast tomorrow, before we head off?'

'I've been here a week…'

'Cecelia, my mother would have had you over the first day if she'd had her own way. I have been the one keeping things separate…'

'Why?'

'Because that's what I always do,' Luka said, and then added, 'And because I was angry.'

They walked on.

'But I can't keep my worlds separate now,' Luka said.

'We have a daughter. My mother has a grandchild...'
He looked at her. 'What about your aunt and uncle? Do
they know about me?'

'No.' Cecelia shook her head. 'They would have had
me straight over to a lawyer,' Cecelia said. 'And then
they'd have gushed all over us both. You were right
about them only taking me on to get to the money.'

She looked out to the cove and the glitter of his yacht
but his wealth was not what beckoned her.

He saw where her gaze fell. 'Do you want to go over
for lunch?' Luka asked.

'No, thank you.' It was hard enough just to walk
alongside him and not break down. She wanted him so
badly and was terrified she'd simply accept whatever
occasional crumbs of affection he threw her way and
so her response was tart. 'I thought the reason I was
here was so you could spend time with your daughter.'

'Believe it or not, I actually have some work to do
today—things were already piling up before my father died.'

'I'm sorry he never got to meet his granddaughter,'
Cecelia said. 'I really do mean that. I feel terrible about
it, in fact...'

'Don't.' Luka shook his head and then turned and
looked at her 'Truth?'

'Please,' she said, and gave a pale smile. He really
was a curious man, for he could so easily have held that
over her. She was surprised to have her guilt so readily dismissed.

'I would not have insisted on a week of playing happy
families had he been alive. I would never have exposed
her to his toxic nature. Instead, I would have brought
Pandora for lunch and that would have been it.'

'I thought the two of you were close.'

'That's what they wanted people to think.'

'Tell me…' Cecelia said, because she simply could not feign disinterest.

'Over dinner.' He nodded to the yacht. 'It's a nice place to talk and I'm not here by accident, Cecelia. My mother has asked if she can have Cecelia stay with her tonight.'

'Absolutely not.' Cecelia shook her head. 'I've given you as much time as you want with her but she is not spending the night away from me. There's no need for your mother to babysit.'

'But she would not be *babysitting*—she is family.' Luka closed his eyes in exasperation. 'She wants to have her granddaughter stay over and to boast to her friends. It's the Greek way.'

She could feel her panic building. It was irrational really, for she wanted Pandora to be surrounded by people who loved her, yet she could not bear the thought of her waking in the dark alone.

'Cecelia, do you really think I would leave Pandora with someone I did not absolutely trust?'

Of course not.

Cecelia knew that.

He had told her that.

And she knew that this was the future.

Time spent away from her daughter as Pandora spent time with people who loved her.

'Roula will be there too,' Luka said. 'Cecelia, I am sure most first-time mothers are anxious when they leave their baby for the first night, but that is co-parenting.'

'I know.'

She swallowed.

It sounded so odd to hear those words from him.

She had honestly thought he would have no interest in Pandora. Or, perhaps the odd visit. Cecelia had genuinely believed he would throw money at the situation.

Instead, Luka wanted to be a true parent. He wanted real time with his daughter and he wanted his family involved in her life.

He just didn't want *her*.

Only that wasn't entirely the case.

Luka turned so he was facing her and when she didn't do the same, he took her shoulders and moved her to face him.

'I want to take you to the yacht tonight because I think it's time that we speak about us.'

'Us?' An incredulous laugh shot from her lips. 'What us? You hate me, and I can't stand the way you live your life—'

'Yet we are parents together,' Luka interrupted. 'And for the record, I don't hate you, and I think you are referring to my former life.'

She assumed he meant prior to him finding out he was a parent.

For Luka, though, the anger was fading, and he was remembering how much he had missed Cecelia this past year.

And now the red mist of anger was clearing, he knew that what he felt for Cecelia had not changed.

Still, he was aware that he could be bullish and knew that to push her too fast would be wrong. She was as jumpy as a cat and a new mother too.

'Cecelia, before the world finds out we have a daughter, I think we should use that time to explore where we stand.'

'I'm not with you.'

'The desire is still there.'

He stated it as fact.

And it was.

Her nails were digging into her palms just from the effort of facing him calmly—the impact of Luka close up was as devastating now as it had been on the day they'd met.

'Perhaps, but sex isn't much to build a relationship on.'

'Why not?' Luka shrugged. 'We both enjoy it and it got us this far.'

She was about to say no but Luka would not be put off.

'Tonight we are going out on our first date.'

Second, she wanted to correct, for her birthday last year had been the most romantic night of her life.

CHAPTER FOURTEEN

THE SPA WAS gorgeous and perhaps more than a little overdue.

Instead of more foils, Cecelia had some length cut off, so that her strawberry blonde hair fell to just below her shoulders, and because it was shorter it coiled into waves.

'How about adding some more waves and wearing it down?' the hairdresser said, but Cecelia shook her head and asked for it to be straightened and put up.

There was an almost imperceptive tut from the hairdresser but she did as asked and smoothed it out and pinned it up.

Though her hair was redder than before, Cecelia felt a small sense of order returning to her world as she eyed her reflection, for she looked more like the Cecelia during her Kargas Holdings days.

Returning to the villa, she took for ever to choose what to wear—everything was too loose and to her mind too sensual.

It isn't work, though, she reminded herself as she found her hand linger upon the sheer rose-gold silk dress.

But it may well be work for Luka.

He adored Pandora, and she was terrified that he

might be merely attempting to do the right thing by his daughter. Cecelia doubted that even his best intentions could last.

She came upon the requisite little black dress and decided it was safer and closer to her usual fare. For a splash of colour she added a little sheer grey silk cardigan that she had packed herself—a throwback from her working days.

She looked at the birthday necklace and wondered if she should wear it, for it was absolutely her favourite thing.

Yet she did not want him to know that he meant everything to her. Luka had made a chance for them sound like a grim reality they ought to face.

Even as he came to her door, Cecelia was holding onto her heart.

Luka was immaculate in a suit and tie, and he had, did, and always would, take her breath away.

'You look very beautiful,' Luka duly said as she closed the door on the villa and they walked towards the speedboat that would take them out to his yacht.

Yet somehow it felt rather like heading to a formal work dinner than a romantic date. And Luka noted she was wearing another damned cardigan.

'How's Pandora?' Cecelia asked, for it felt like for ever since she had seen her. But if tonight didn't work then being apart from her daughter for prolonged stretches was something she would have to get used to.

Yes, there was an awful lot of pressure on this date.

'She is being spoiled by her *yia-yia* and also her great-aunt, my father's sister,' Luka said, and he took out his phone and showed her a photo he had taken just before he left.

If ever there was a baby who was doted on it was

Pandora. She had on a cerise dress and was a splash of gorgeousness between the two doting women dressed in black.

'My mother is so happy and relaxed. I cannot tell you the balm that our daughter is to her.'

As she boarded his stunning yacht, Cecelia couldn't help but think of all the wild debauched parties that had taken place here.

Tonight, though, there weren't the half-naked, sun-kissed and oiled bodies, or the pulse of music to dance to. And there was only one champagne cork that popped and no raucous laughter.

It wasn't so much his past that she loathed, more the certainty that he would tire of her and go back to it someday.

It was a gorgeous night, the sky as navy as Pandora's eyes and pierced with endless stars.

The deck was romantically lit and it was soft music that greeted her as they were led to a beautifully dressed table.

The waiter placed her napkin in her lap and Cecelia did her absolute best to relax.

They ate the best squid she had ever tasted—or *ka-lamari*, as the waiter called it—and she looked out at Xanero and saw the gorgeous buildings from her view on the water.

'It really is the most beautiful place,' Cecelia said.

'It has been both a blessing and a curse,' Luka said. 'It's a blessing now.'

'You mean now that your father's gone?' Cecelia tentatively asked, alluding to what he had said on the beach.

He nodded. 'My mother would say I should not speak ill of the dead, but there is nothing good that I can say about him. He was work-shy and a bully...'

'I thought you and he worked together in the restaurant, that he passed on all he knew.'

'He probably put in twelve hours tops in his entire lifetime,' Luka said. 'But my mother had always wanted a family business. I could have had him removed, but she pleaded with me not to. It was easier to stay away and run it from a distance.' He looked out across the water and then he told her something he could not explain, even to himself. 'And yet his death has rocked my world and I feel like I'm grieving.'

'I still grieve for my mother,' she admitted. 'Sometimes I think I miss what could have been.'

And then her eyes flicked away because, although they were talking about their parents, she was suddenly thinking of them and what *might* be, perhaps.

'I want you to love it here too,' Luka said, and she put down her fork. 'You've had a good week?' he asked.

'It's been better than I thought it would be.'

'There could be many more.'

'There's no could about it.' She looked at him and reminded herself who she was dealing with. 'Given that you've told me to be here one week a month or you'll see me in court.'

'I meant *this*, Cecelia. Us.' He saw her jaw tighten but he reached across the table and took her hand. It was as rigid as ever, her professional façade still in place. Yet as he toyed with her, she found her fingers intertwining with his and then he voiced her thoughts exactly.

'I'm going crazy, knowing you're here but not in my bed.'

He watched as her eyes screwed closed and assumed he had pushed too hard when in truth Cecelia was also fighting desire.

'We don't have to rush things,' he corrected, 'but maybe when you bring Pandora here, when there is no chance of us being seen, then away from prying eyes we can date, get to know each other, see how we work as a family…'

She felt like the only car in the showroom about to be taken on a reluctant test drive. 'And if we don't work?' she asked.

'Cecelia….'

'No, Luka, what you're basically proposing is that I be your mistress during the time Pandora and I are here in Xanero.'

'What I'm proposing is that we give us a try. I'm going to attempt to let go of the fact that you kept Pandora from me…'

'You're never going to forgive me for that, are you?'

'I don't know,' he admitted.

It killed her to hear that for it gave them such a lousy start and so she kicked back. 'Can you really blame me for not telling you?' Cecelia could no longer hold it in. 'Have you any idea the hell you put me through, dealing with all your cast-offs? I was crazy about you and you were into everyone but me!'

'And you didn't think to tell me?'

'You were my boss then!'

'Well, I'm not now.'

'No, but it's no better here, knowing what went on aboard this yacht and by the bloody pool…'

'Don't turn this around on me. You never gave me a single indication you were interested in me. In fact, you were engaged when I first hired you. I'm damned if I do and damned if I don't. You were the one in a serious relationship, remember?'

'And you were the one screwing around.' She flung

down her napkin and there was the scrape of her chair as she stood. 'I need to get back.'

'We need to speak.' Luka took her wrist.

'No, I want to get off...'

'Fine.'

He snapped his fingers to prepare the speedboat that would take them back to shore. 'Do you know something,' Luka said. 'I'm sick and tired of seeing the disproval in your eyes...'

'Well, someone has to be responsible,' she spat.

'And you elect yourself at every turn.'

'Because I'm scared that if I let go, then I might turn into my mother!' she shouted.

'Cecelia...' he was about to tell her that she was being ridiculous but then he looked at it from her side, the chaotic upbringing, the uncertainty, the abandonment. 'You will never be her. And I promise you this, the day you hit the cocaine, I shall put you over my knee...'

She almost laughed.

Almost.

But her throat was thick with tears.

'We're in this together,' Luka said. 'Did she leave you at night?'

'Many times.' Cecelia nodded. 'I would wake up and not know where she was. That's why I don't want Pandora—'

'The difference is,' Luka cut in, 'that, though it might not be her mother she wakes to, she will have family there, or a nanny who has been carefully chosen. Cecelia, there's a world of difference between having a night out and living the life your mother lived.' But Cecelia turned away and he shook his head for she would never see it from his point of view. 'We'll go and fetch her now.'

As the boat sped them to shore, Cecelia felt like an utter failure—back from a romantic night out before ten. As he helped her onto the pier she did not know how to explain it—she knew he was right, that Pandora was safe and loved, but it was about more than just that. 'Luka, you don't have to wake her. Leave her with your mother and Roula. I know she'll be fine.'

'Are you sure?'

Cecelia nodded.

'You're a wonderful mother, Cecelia.'

But as a lover she knew she had failed.

The night was over for them.

'Luka,' she tried to explain how she felt, 'I'm scared of us getting together and confusing her when we break up...'

'How about *if* we break up?' Luka asked. 'How about we don't ever break up? You're so bloody negative and contained.'

'Because the one time I lived a little, look what happened! The one time I made a mist—'

She stopped there because she didn't ever want to describe Pandora and what had happened as a mistake because she wasn't.

But Luka got there first. 'The one time you let your hair down and lived a little, to my mind, something rather beautiful happened.'

And then he looked down at her and he was angry, for she had refused on so many occasions to give them a chance.

'Cecelia, I'm not going to beg. You have to want it too.'

CHAPTER FIFTEEN

LUKA STRODE OFF.

She watched him walk angrily along the beach and she knew it was she who had messed up the night.

Yet the cheek of him!

On-call sex whenever she was here?

Or, a little voice to her heart said, could it serve as the start of being a real family?

Cecelia was terrified of loving him.

Yet she already did.

More, she was terrified of admitting to loving him and then losing him.

Of waking in the dark and it being *him* that was gone.

Or, worse, the cold pretence of normal, and pretending there was love, as her uncle and aunt had done.

Sex was all they had and when that novelty dimmed he would be back to his old life....

She walked along the white sandy beach, straying a little from the boundaries of the complex. This would be home for a while, she realised.

Not all the time, but for a year or so she would be here for a week every month.

And then not at all.

She was terrified to enjoy it and relax into it, knowing all the while that it would all soon be taken away from her.

He would always be there for Pandora, though.

She was starting to believe that things would be different for her daughter than they had been for her. That, despite her carelessness that one morning, she had chosen well for he was proving to be an amazing father—completely rearranging his world to accommodate his daughter.

'Live a little.'

She recalled his words as he had moved her little pottery jar and then she winced as she remembered her *No, thank you* response.

She remembered him throwing her into the pool and then joining her, his eyes imploring her to loosen up and be free.

He had been offering a chance for them, and rather than embrace that chance she was hiding from it. Rather than living the life she wanted to with him, she was running from it at every turn.

Yet Luka was right, the one time she had let her hair down and lived a little, something rather beautiful had happened.

She recalled his words. *'You have to want it too.'*

Oh, she did, she very much did, and she had to show him that somehow.

And so instead of heading back to the villa to spend the night feeling sorry for herself, Cecelia decided it was time to head out.

While she did head back to the villa it was only to change. She peeled off the cardigan and little black dress and instead of flesh-coloured knickers and a bra, she pulled on the rose-gold bikini.

For she might want a midnight swim!

She thought of Luka naked and wet and dripping water over her, as had been her fantasy for so long.

Over the bikini she pulled on the rose-gold dress that was so loose and flowing, and yet so sensual.

Her hair when she took it down was wavy and wild thanks to the salt spray of the ocean.

Her cheeks were flushed and her green eyes finally had their sparkle back after a week of doing nothing and actually sleeping.

Or did it have more to do with a week spent closer to him?

There could be many more weeks, if she had the courage to try....

A monthly tryst with Luka didn't sound so terrible now. They were like a little family, and being together in the pool once a month, rather than her lying lonely poolside on the other side of the complex, would be much better, wouldn't it?

Pandora would have the best mother, the best co-parents—and if Luka couldn't forgive her for not telling him about their baby that was his right.

She put on the necklace, the one he had given her and the one she would adore for ever, feeling the cold metal against her heated skin. Then Cecelia headed to the restaurant she had never so much as visited, preferring instead to hide away in the villa.

It was stunning and, yes, full of couples, but there at the bar was Luka, with his back to her.

'Your table is ready for you, Madam,' the greeter said, and she recalled it had been reserved for her all week.

The bar manager told Luka that Cecelia had arrived. He frowned, glanced over and saw that she was being seated—only it was not a Cecelia he recognised.

Well, perhaps the one he met at times in his dreams, for she looked amazing and relaxed and sexy too as she laughed at something the greeter said.

He looked over but she did not catch his eye. He was trying to work out what was going on when the bar manager spoke and placed in front of him a glass of the best champagne.

'Gia eséna kýrie, apó tin kyría.' For you, sir, from the lady.

And it was like in days of old, but so much better now. As he turned, Cecelia met his eyes and raised her own glass, adding a slight gesture of her head.

A gesture that invited Luka to join her.

She smiled a slow smile that was familiar from many years ago.

A flirt.

An offer.

Yes, Cecelia was a curious mix indeed, for never would he have envisaged this.

He walked over, his eyes never leaving her face. 'It's far too nice a night to drink champagne alone,' Luka said.

'I agree,' she said. 'Would you care to join me?'

'I would love to.'

He took a seat and looked over at a woman who had, from the day they had met, intrigued him. Never more so than now, and he slipped so easily back into the game. 'How long are you here for?'

'I fly back to London tomorrow,' she said. 'Although I believe it won't be the last time I'm here.'

'That's good to know,' Luka said. 'And are you here alone?'

'It's a little complicated, I don't really want to go into it.'

'That's fine.'

But this time it was not disapproval in her eyes, for it was like he was back staring into that aurora and he started to understand her some more. There was a wild side to Cecelia, one she had fought all her life to temper.

Not tonight.

She *could* be free around him.

'I have a daughter,' she said, 'but she's being taken care of tonight.'

'So you're on your own.'

'Yes,' Cecelia said. 'All night.'

'Poor you.' He gave her a smile, the one that had churned her heart since the day they'd met. 'I didn't catch your name.'

'Cece.'

He smiled that slow smile that made her stomach fold.

'I'm Luka. So, where are you staying.'

'At the Beach Side apartment.'

'Nice,' he said.

'Very.' She took a sip of champagne and then smirked. 'My ex is paying.'

'Even better,' he said, and then Luka laughed and it was the most delicious sound she had ever heard.

But then he met her eyes and his voice was serious. 'He must be a fool to have let you go.'

'Not really,' Cecelia said. 'I let him down.'

'I doubt it,' he said.

'Oh, but I did. I kept something very important from him.'

'Then he should have got over it, or perhaps he should have taken the time to work out why you did what you did.'

He saw a flash of tears and decided that there would be no tears now.

'I shouldn't really be seen drinking in the restaurant with a guest,' Luka said. He held her eyes and the tears dispersed like a chink in the mist.

'Then come back to mine.'

It was the bravest thing she had done and he was so deliciously casual in his response.

'Sure, though for the sake of discretion, you should leave first.'

She would never not want him, Cecelia knew as she stood to go, but he caught her wrist.

'Is there anything you'd like?' he asked. 'Anything at all?'

He was inviting her to name her wants.

This she did.

Cecelia bent over and whispered into his ear and then pulled back, wondering at his reaction and if he might laugh at her request, but he just nodded.

'No problem.'

She felt as if she was on a high as she arrived back at the villa.

A dizzy high and, yes, it might just be sex but she would take it if it afforded them a start.

She did not turn on the lights. Instead, she slipped off her clothes and lay on the bed. Her body felt as though it might burst into flames of desire as she lay there.

Waiting.

Not wondering as to their future, not berating herself with the impossibility of it all, just waiting for her night with him.

She heard the splash from the pool and closed her eyes as she listened to him move through the water and then she caught the slide of the villa doors.

And then, dripping wet, he leaned over her.

As per her request.

She felt the mattress indent as he knelt over her and relished the cold drops of water on her skin. 'I want you, Cece...' he told her. His mouth found hers and she closed her eyes to the bliss of his kiss. 'I've been crazy about you for so long.'

His voice was raw with want, and even if he was simply saying it for this night of fantasy, even if he simply knew how to pleasure women through years of practice, she didn't care just so long as this night he pleasured her.

His kiss tasted of salty ocean water and his body was cold and wet while hers burnt beneath him.

'There's been no one since you,' he told her. He broke the fantasy a little, yet she ached for it to be true and in response she gave in to his kiss.

His tongue was tender yet probing and she could feel his erection between her thighs. She yearned for him to enter her, yet he held back.

'I'm on the Pill,' she told him.

'That costs more, lady,' he teased. He made her laugh and he joined her, and then he stopped laughing and took her arms, which were wrapped around him, and held them above her head, so that she could not move, and could only look at him.

'I love you,' he told her, and she closed her eyes.

'Luka, don't.'

'Look at me,' he said, and she did.

'I love you.'

He was tired of holding back, tired of denying it.

'Please, please, don't just say it,' she begged. No matter how much she yearned to hear it, she could not stand that it might be a game and mere words delivered from silken lips by a man who knew what to say.

'But I do,' Luka said. He was starting to realise that Cece did need him to call the shots, and now he knew why and he went back to their conversation in the restaurant, when she had referred to him as her ex. 'Perhaps your ex should have understood that for you it's hard to believe someone might love you, when no one ever has before.'

He was so right, and so for a moment she allowed herself the bliss of believing he did as Luka took her deeply.

He moaned with relief as he slipped inside, and she gave in to bliss, to the dream that his love was hers and that the body that moved over and within her might be hers for ever.

Eyes open, she watched as he moved with her, each stroke of him inside bringing her nearer to a peak, and she gave in to his kiss and shattered to his bliss.

'Cece...' he groaned as he spilled inside her. There could be no place better than this.

In this still, dark place on a sultry night, she fell asleep in his arms and pretended this was love.

CHAPTER SIXTEEN

'I MEANT WHAT I said,' Luka told her.

She woke to his words and found he was spooned in behind her. His hand moved from her breast as he played with the stones of her necklace.

They were rubies, not glass, and way too much of a gift for a PA.

A mixed message indeed, even for him, for when it had finally arrived in his life, Luka had not recognised love either.

'Why couldn't you tell me how you felt, Cece?'

'Because so many woman have made fools of themselves over you and I didn't want to be another one of them.'

He could not argue with that.

'If it wasn't for Pandora,' Cecelia said, still facing away, 'there would be no us.'

'Had you been walking in the street that day alone, I would have called you. And,' Luka added, 'when my father died, it was you I wanted to reach out to. I told myself to wait. To get through the funeral and clear my head. I told myself I wasn't thinking straight, but I was lying because since that night with you things have never been clearer. There's been no one since you.'

She hadn't believed him when he'd told her that last

night. Cecelia had thought he was just saying the words she wanted to hear.

'I think I loved you back then but, hell, Cece, you made it hard to get close. All I can say was I loathed the thought of you being gone.'

She was starting to believe that there might be a chance for them, but her mind knew only how to doubt.

'Even if we try to make a go of it, one day you'll throw it back in my face that I kept Pandora from you...'

'Would the world end if I did?' Luka asked. He guessed that from the way life had treated her, or rather *people* had treated her, that, yes, it would seem that way to her.

He smiled that rare smile and she glimpsed a future, one where he tossed her flaw in her face and it did not end them.

'No.'

'And when—if—I do hurl it at you, perhaps you will remind me of the many women I bedded, and the flowers you ordered on my behalf, and what an ass I was...'

'Yes,' she said, torn between laughing and crying.

It was a love where perfection was not a prerequisite, one where you were allowed to mess up.

'Marry me, Cece.'

She sat up in bed and wasn't certain what she'd just heard. 'I thought we were going to take things slowly. I'll be back in a few weeks...'

'If you think I am letting you get on a plane this morning, then you don't know me at all.'

She turned and smiled.

It was the smile that felt like summer to him.

'Do you know what day it is?'

Cecelia shook her head.

'It's your birthday...'

But this year it wasn't candles and cake, or a neck-lace she was gifted with, but a ring.

'Were you going to ask me last night?' Cecelia gasped, as he slipped a huge diamond on her finger, faint with horror for her handling of things.

But she didn't know him completely yet, for Luka shook his head.

'No, it was always meant for this morning, because I don't want you ever to have another birthday that passed unnoticed.'

Sometimes she thought he just said the right thing, the things she wanted to hear. But this didn't feel like that. This felt real somehow.

'Come on, then!' He kicked off the sheet. 'We've a wedding to get to.'

'We can't just get married.' Cecelia laughed. 'We need approval, and what about guests and—?'

'I practically own the island,' Luka pointed out. 'I can do what I want, we can deal with the legalities later. I might just have to marry you again, but I want a wedding ring on your finger today and,' he added, 'it's never coming off.'

'But what about Pandora?'

'Where I come from, children don't generally attend their parents' wedding,' Luka said. 'Had you bothered to tell me you were pregnant we could have sorted it out and we'd have been married many months ago and Pandora wouldn't come from a broken home.'

He was throwing it all back in her face, yet she smiled.

'Luka, I don't have anything to wear.'

'Then I'll marry you in a sheet, but, Cece...' he took her arms and pinned her down, staring right into her eyes '...you have to want it too.'

'I do.'

'And you have to fight for us as well,' he said, and then halted, for she was the one who had fought for them last night. He thought of her, so shy and reserved, yet she had walked into the restaurant, and somehow forgiven his past. 'You're going to marry me now and then we're going to collect out daughter together. As a married couple, as her parents…'

Cecelia wore a silver sarong tied over one shoulder. Her hair was strawberry blonde and curly as she stood on the yacht and faced Luka.

He wore black dress pants and a fitted white shirt but no tie and he had not shaved.

It was informal, yet beautiful and impulsive too.

Yes, she might be a little more than just a visual replica of her mother, for the wanton side of her nature appeared at times. But though a sudden wedding aboard Luka Kargas's yacht might appear reckless to some, Cecelia knew that she stood before a man who was strong and who loved her.

And who would not let her fall.

The celebrant looked up at the sound of a helicopter buzzing overhead, and suggested that perhaps they move inside if they wanted to avoid being photographed.

'Sure,' Luka said, for he wanted to shield her, but as he went to take her hand and move below deck, she declined.

'It's fine.' Cecelia gave a little shake of her head. 'It will save us having to announce it.'

With him she was both brave and free.

'I love you,' he told her as he slid a wedding band on her finger. 'And if it takes the rest of my life to prove it to you, I will.'

'You already have,' Cecelia said, and then she looked into velvet brown eyes that were black when guarded. She knew him better than anyone else, and so she told him a truth. 'And I'm so proud to be your wife.'

She was.

Cecelia was proud not just of the man he was but the man he had been, for he had been strong in the face of an impossible start in life.

It meant everything to Luka to hear that.

The press got one shot—Luka Kargas on his yacht, kissing his bride, but by the time the paparazzi had got wind of the news and circled ahead, awaiting the pulse of music and wild celebrations, the happy couple had long since left.

They had somewhere else they wanted to be.

Cecelia walked up the path towards her mother-in-law's villa, feeling more than a little nervous, and saw Sophie sitting in a chair, holding Pandora. Beside them was a large silver box and a birthday and wedding breakfast awaiting.

The late-morning sun was high in the sky and there was peace in the air as they returned to their daughter… a family at last.

* * * * *

MILLS & BOON

Coming next month

KIDNAPPED FOR HIS ROYAL DUTY

Jane Porter

Before they came to Jolie, Dal would have described Poppy as pretty, in a fresh, wholesome, no-nonsense sort of way with her thick, shoulder-length brown hair and large, brown eyes and a serious little chin.

But as Poppy entered the dining room with its glossy white ceiling and dark purple walls, she looked anything but wholesome and no-nonsense.

She was wearing a silk gown the color of cherries, delicately embroidered with silver threads, and instead of her usual ponytail or chignon, her dark hair was down, and long, elegant chandelier earrings dangled from her ears. As she walked, the semi-sheer kaftan molded to her curves.

"It seems I've been keeping you waiting," she said, her voice pitched lower than usual and slightly breathless. "Izba insisted on all this," she added, gesturing up toward her face.

At first Dal thought she was referring to the ornate silver earrings that were catching and reflecting the light, but once she was seated across from him he realized her eyes had been rimmed with kohl and her lips had been outlined and filled in with a soft plum-pink gloss. "You're wearing makeup."

"Quite a lot of it, too." She grimaced. "I tried to explain to Izba that this wasn't me, but she's very determined once she makes her mind up about something and apparently, dinner with you requires me to look like a tart."

Dal checked his smile. "You don't look like a tart. Unless it's the kind of tart one wants to eat."

Color flooded Poppy's cheeks and she glanced away, suddenly shy, and he didn't know if it was her shyness or the shimmering dress that clung to her, but he didn't think any woman could be more beautiful, or desirable than Poppy right now. "You look lovely," he said quietly. "But I don't want you uncomfortable all through dinner. If you'd rather go remove the makeup I'm happy to wait."

She looked at him closely as if doubting his sincerity. "It's fun to dress up, but I'm worried Izba has the wrong idea about me."

"And what is that?"

"She seems to think you're going to...marry...me."

Continue reading
KIDNAPPED FOR HIS ROYAL DUTY
Jane Porter

Available next month
www.millsandboon.co.uk

LET'S TALK
Romance

For exclusive extracts, competitions
and special offers, find us online:

f facebook.com/millsandboon

📷 @millsandboonuk

🛡 @millsandboon

Or get in touch on 0844 844 1351*

For all the latest titles coming soon, visit
millsandboon.co.uk/nextmonth

Want even more
ROMANCE?

Join our bookclub today!

'Mills & Boon books, the perfect way to escape for an hour or so.'

Miss W. Dyer

'Excellent service, promptly delivered and very good subscription choices.'

Miss A. Pearson

'You get fantastic special offers and the chance to get books before they hit the shops.'

Mrs V. Hall

Visit millsandboon.co.uk/Bookclub
and save on brand new books.

MILLS & BOON